LOOK AT ME

Look At Me

A Novel By

Lauren Porosoff Mitchell

Leapfrog Press
Wellfleet, Massachusetts

Published in 2000 in the United States by
The Leapfrog Press
P.O. Box 1495   95 Commercial Street
Wellfleet, MA 02667-1495, USA
www.leapfrogpress.com

Distributed in the United States by
Consortium Book Sales and Distribution
St. Paul, Minnesota 55114

First Edition

Library of Congress Cataloging-in-Publication Data

Mitchell, Lauren Porosoff, 1975-
    Look at me : a novel / by Lauren Porosoff Mitchell. – 1st ed.
    p. cm.
    ISBN 0-9654578-1-8 (pbk. : alk. paper)
        1. Mothers—Death—Psychological aspects—Fiction.
        2. Mothers and daughters—Fiction.
        3. Young women—Fiction. I. Title.

PS3563.I76765 L66 2000
813'.6—dc21

                                                    00-028747

            10 9 8 7 6 5 4 3 2 1

Printed in the United States of America

To my wonderful husband Larry Mitchell,
Who looked and saw,
And for whom I wrote this book without knowing it.

A Note of Introduction

We began Leapfrog Press with the idea of publishing out-of-print favorites as well as new works by established writers and those just starting out. While we've covered each category in the few short years we've been in business, it was with some surprise that the category we included last, and which we assumed we'd publish the least of, has given us so much pleasure to produce. Publishing *leo@fergusrules.com* by Arne Tangherlini, seemed to open the floodgates to an outpouring of new submissions by first novelists that we could not ignore and which has become an exciting direction for Leapfrog, one in which we'll be introducing bright new talent.

Look At Me is a fresh, edgy, sexy first novel by a young woman still in law school. It is a frank story of promiscuity, of the clash and intermingling of sex and love, of the struggle with and acceptance of family legacy.

The style moves from the matter-of-fact to magic realism as Lauren Porosoff Mitchell explores the adventures and the mind of her protagonist, Dana.

Dana's childhood is evoked for us, her loving and charismatic mother with some of the powers of a witch, and her father, the super rational scientist. Her parents had a passionate marriage abruptly broken by the mother's death far too young. Dana is caught between the different pulls of her mother and her father. She is a geneticist, a scientist like her father, but her life outside of work is far from rational and controlled, and far from the warm nurturing atmosphere her mother created. As Dana puts it, "a man of science wedded to a sorceress"—what kind of daughter indeed can issue from such a mixed heritage?

Since childhood, sex for Dana is as much a matter of control as pleasure—her ability to *pull* men toward her as her mother could *pull* objects through the air and her ability to dismiss them when the brief adventure is completed to her satisfaction. She is comfortable with the 'slut' side of her nature, but less so with her own desire for love. Love frightens her unless she can build it into a myth she controls. She has a compulsion to prove her ability to attract, again and again, but the objects of her conquest lose their own desirability quickly.

This is an odyssey through Washington D.C., through clubs and coffee houses, through bookstores and airports, through actual and imaginary flying, through drugs and the mornings-after of a young woman trying to understand her past and her present and to grapple with the contradictory urges and needs she finds in herself and acts out.

Since childhood, Dana has felt herself a sort of freak who could not easily make friends with other women or with men. She has used sex to grab attention and to relieve her loneliness while leaving it intact afterward. As a woman scientist, as a sexual aggressor, as someone without emotional ties, she finds herself still as much an outsider as the little girl whose imagination took her into other realities when school bored her.

After all the faceless men who service her for a night and whom she expels with a well-worked out routine in the morning, she meets two who compel her attention, whom she cannot dismiss: Jonas, the married astronomer from San Francisco she meets on a plane and cannot forget; and Iain, a photographer with a cocaine addiction and dangerous lifestyle, but a man of great compassion and tenderness. Afraid of his gentleness and accessibility, Dana keeps him at arm's length, sorting through the tensions and pleasures of measured friendship while she pursues Jonas and the memory of an extraordinary night in an observatory where she could not remain the detached observer and indeed saw stars.

Dana is a contemporary young woman, at home with her sexuality but at odds with her emotions. Her quest will strike a chord with many her age who are struggling to understand their own identities and desires. *Look At Me* will also illuminate the lives of young people for those of generations whose lives were dissimilar but whose needs were not. It is a striking first novel I was delighted to pull out of all the unsolicited manuscripts that arrive at our press daily. Lauren Porosoff Mitchell is indeed a talent to watch.

—Marge Piercy

Look At Me

ONE

I BROUGHT ANOTHER ONE home tonight. This one had a small birthmark behind his left earlobe and cool skin that smelled of coconut milk and lemon leaves. I catalogue them this way, by the most minor of their physical details, because otherwise they are not prone to distinction. The drink is always the same; though the color varies from pink to clear to amber, its effects are consistent. It convinces him that he is the one luring me away from the bar to a more private place—my bedroom, with its bare walls and white bed, antiseptic as a hospital and well-trafficked as Union Station. But private, yes. The walls of my apartment are insulated, so when I get on top and ride one of the men my neighbors don't hear. I am screaming, grunting. Sweating as my body rhythmically contracts. I rip pleasure out of them, one at a time, evening by evening. And by day I ignore the oily feel of them that does not wash off.

Sometimes I am drunk, and I awaken with a headache to find one of them asleep in my bed, his hair daubed in sweaty clumps to his face. Then I rise from my bed and sit at my laptop in the next room, typing in the dark until the sky bleeds vermilion. It is this light or the clicking keys that wake him; I do not know which. He sees me like that, writing in the morning light, spread out naked with one foot up on either corner of the desk, and I watch as the shame passes through his body. He goes soft. He feels he has violated me somehow, that he has transgressed some essential privacy. I observe with interest as he considers his own voyeurism, and I think every time it is silly, he probably still has the taste of me in his mouth. And yet he is afraid, inadequate, discovering me like this in the dying dark. He puts on his smoke-stinking jeans and sweat-damp polo shirt. He stumbles putting on his expensive sneakers that were flung in the entryway the night before. All the time I watch him. I don't stop watching until he half-kisses me and leaves and shuts the door softly behind him. Only then do I delete the page of *O*s and *J*s and ampersands and percent symbols, make pancakes, and start my work.

As children, we hide under the blanket and the monsters are gone. From the outside, what is visible is a safe heap of comforter, smooth and placid, hiding the child tiny and quivering inside. Night by night we convince ourselves that there are no monsters, until we can sleep serene in our knowledge that we are safe. Pretend we are protected, and the protection becomes real. The monsters cannot hurt you anymore because you deny their power.

There are no monsters, you say? But it is not an act of convincing ourselves that they are false but of enlightening ourselves that they are products of our minds: controllable, secured, innocuous, yes, but only by virtue of being real.

One Saturday afternoon when I was fifteen an older boy from school called me and asked if I wanted to go out. The trees were woven into pale budded webs against a peacock blue sky, the lakes rippled with wind, and I was exuberant in a new skirt and too much lipstick. The boy picked me up in his deteriorating station wagon, drove around for a while listening to his music, then pulled up in front of our school and asked if I wanted to walk around. He took me into the woods behind the school and inserted his crude dirty fingers into my vagina. Then he hoisted me up and fucked me against a big rock that felt rough against my young ass and for days after I had scratches and bruises and I avoided him in the school hallways. Two weeks later one of his best friends called me in the middle of the night and asked me to meet him behind his house and suck his cock. But these boys, these imbecilic boys with their hormones and superiority complexes and competitive inclinations, were unable to see the naked, intractable, and wily girl who seemed ready to pleasure them. Naked I was most beautiful, but they never saw me. They never once looked for what lived in the contours they loved to grope. They saw something, some gathering of shapes and light, but it was not my body. They felt something, time after time, thinking it was my body. But it was not.

So you see, the monsters are real.

Now I wake up, often in a bed damp with the juices of angry lust. I pretend to write until my interloper flees. I make breakfast, write furious words until it is time to go to the science tower at the university and analyze usually flawed genetic material and squelch the hopes of optimistic parents-to-be. I go home, go to the bar, choose another candidate to take home and screw. Sundays I spend in solitude.

Our senses are endlessly deceptive. The visible spectrum of light wavelengths, for example, goes from violet to red, or from 400 to 750 nanometers. We have the words *infrared* and *ultraviolet* to describe colors we cannot see, and beyond those we have trouble imagining what other colors might look like if we could see them. And even with this very limited range of vision, we focus, project, stabilize, and otherwise distort the image, which is saying nothing of how the brain reinterprets it to become something else entirely, a fish into a flower. And we have words, *fish* or *flower* trying to describe this cocktail of images we sense, certain that we see not many things but one, not a gathering of light but a meaningful organism. A child sniffs a peony and says, "Pretty pink flower." Perhaps this is all we are capable of understanding.

We group the world; we like to reduce it to its lowest terms. We swallow it, one tablet of information at a time, rewarded for this effort by seeing a coherent world and one logical line through space-time. And even the psychologists, physicists and poets who are vaguely aware of what exists beyond these parameters can get up, get dressed and have breakfast in the morning without being stunned by the proliferation of brightness.

And certain forms of madness involve not being able to think straight. We are used to the one line; we call it by reassuring names like sobriety and sanity. Those who feel the weight of its limits try hallucinogenic drugs to experience the world beyond this line, but really these worlds they conjure are only a different distortion. We taste the real world, oddly enough, only in faint, almost imperceptible brushes with imagination. And if you look at it with your eyes, it vanishes like an afterimage or a ghost.

I would like to be able to tell you to trust me, but this is my version of the story. And while I know now that he was not one of my characters, I warn you that I have never learned to convey what is real, that even if I experienced him as real I extrude something else, and again you see it differently. So do not trust me but listen anyway. It began on a train.

"So? Are you the devil incarnate?"

He has been leaning casually on a kiosk at the metro. I have been watching him, trying to be discreet. He steps onto the red line train with the grace of a glittering Pavlova, sits red-eyed in the first row. The train is empty. From the wide selection of seats I choose the one perpendicular to his, so that when I cross my legs and my long black dress slides up to my thigh, the bare white skin almost touches him.

"What?" He is hazy, but his ice-blue eyes have been fixed on me, though he has been trying not to allow me to notice. The hot breath of the train saturates the subway car as its doors open for the next station.

It may be that he has been crying, hard, all day, but I suspect drugs. Marijuana probably, maybe even cocaine. His body is air-spun, made of nothing, and to cover this wispy presence he is wearing thin fraying jeans and a shirt printed with Sanskrit letters and a hammered metal necklace, on which is mounted a tiny paper bearing the words that are the subject of my inquiry.

"Your necklace. It says 'the devil incarnate.' Are you?" I am being more flirtatious now. From my inventory of voices I have selected the quiet one with a provisional innocence veiling what I know they know is a lurid interior.

"Oh," and he fidgets with the pendant. "My friend made this for me. She sells jewelry at the Eastern Market. I work there too, some weekends. Sundays."

"I can't believe I've never noticed you. I go to the Market sometimes."

The small talk that ensues is not important. By definition, it is small. What is important is the way he stares at me with huge, blue, bloodshot eyes. The way I cross and re-cross my legs, seeming carefree but being absolutely sure that the fabric of my long, black cotton dress comes up over my knees. I fidget with my red hair, with the amber of my necklace, with the hem of my dress laid across my knee. He tells me about his photography classes at the university and his dreams of traveling to India, but his voice is so hesitant and the train so loud that I only hear occasional disembodied words.

The metro groans at every stop, and soon I am pulling my cellular out of my purse and apologizing for having to use it. I call Garrett to tell him to leave for the station. He will pick me up there and take me to Baltimore to walk around the harbor and look at the boats. He will try to show off his knowledge by asking the Marines on board questions about the craft. I probably won't fuck Garrett.

"Of course, you have a date," says the blue-eyed saint whose combat-boot-covered instep touches my knee, lightly. His voice is deliberate now but soft, as if the person speaking is not in fact next to me on the train but very far away and trying to ensure, futilely, that I understand every word.

"Yes." I say it with resignation. I look at him, and this is the moment I begin loving him, an experience that has not ended since.

That could have been the last exchange between us. I could have gotten off the metro car, ridden the escalator down to where Garrett and I would meet and forgotten all about this delicate boy who had held me as if by telekinesis. But no, no, I would walk the city seeking him. Not all the time, of course, but whenever I rode the metro or happened to think of him, I would look around desperately as if cornered at a party or lost in a parking lot. Where are you? Why didn't I heed my instinct and accompany you to your stop and follow you to wherever you were bound? I started going every weekend to the Eastern Market, entranced by the smells of basil plants and tomato leaves, enthralled by the sea-glass earrings and wooden beads and pale watercolor paintings at all the tables, but I did not see the jewelry with the words, and I did not see the boy.

Once when my mother was alive, she took me for a walk to a marble bench draped in wisteria. It was a numinous place, and she told me she used to go past it on her daily walk when she was pregnant with me. On the bench, she said, there often sat a woman, old and crazed, wrapped in dusty clothing that left exposed only her round, softly wrinkled face. This woman was there every day for months, but after Mama gave birth to me the woman stopped appearing.

"She was my angel," Mama said. Odd words for a Jewish woman to her only child, I knew even then, but I

19

trusted all of her senses.

At the Market I glanced around hopefully, but no. Perhaps the boy was my impalpable angel, my encounter with him nothing more than (nothing less than?) a vision. I too needed protection because of what lived inside me.

One Sunday at the Market, wandering in my usual haze from table to table, I saw an array of hammered metal pendants and charms with words affixed and enameled on. "Delicious," said one, and another, "wonderland." I was holding up "luminary" when the slight, blond girl behind the table asked if she could help me with something.

"Actually, yes," I said, looking her in the eye, flirting as much with her as with anyone who has something I want. I proceeded to describe my encounter with the saint and requested her help in finding him.

"I think you're talking about Iain. That sounds like the kind of thing that would happen to him."

"Iain," I pronounced his name, feeling it start in the back of my throat and end in a vibration behind my front teeth. "I didn't even know his name until this moment. I'm Dana, by the way."

"I'm Jo," she said, extending her hand. "If you want to write him a note, I'd be happy to deliver it. I'll see him at Sepia on Tuesday."

"Sepia?"

"It's a bookstore in upper Georgetown. Iain and I work there together."

Eagerly I produced a pad of paper and a runny blue pen from my shoulder bag and began writing in a hand as slow and deliberate as Iain's voice.

Look at Me

Dear Iain,

My name is Dana. When we met on the red line I did not get a chance to tell you that because I was too scared, and I have regretted that decision since. I hope you remember me, even though our meeting was brief. I have long dark red hair and pale skin, and I was wearing a black dress and an amber necklace. You looked tired. We joked about Baltimore and knot-tying and the Scarsdale diet. You told me your longings. Maybe we can meet again. I understand if you think this is too weird and you don't want to respond, but I hope you will.

I signed the letter and wrote my telephone number at the bottom, then folded the paper and presented it to Jo.

"I promise I won't read it," she said, slipping the paper into a plastic bag meant for packaging the jewelry she sold. "And I know how you feel. Sometimes the connection is strong, even when logic says it shouldn't be."

"It leads to some pretty strange behaviors, doesn't it? I'll take 'luminary.' How much?"

I should be describing Jo but the details of her are frivolous. Her role in my history was merely as a messenger bird. I gave her the twelve dollars for the necklace and a peony by way of thanks and said goodbye.

Then I would wait.

It makes a nice story, doesn't it? And what happens next? Do they find each other? Of course, of course. The lovers meet at some crowded location in the city, a nightclub perhaps, or at a metro station, to make an elegant parallel to their first encounter. She is looking the other way when he spots her, alone and vulnerable and wearing a necklace to match the one he has not taken off since the day it brought her to him. Shy as he approaches her, so timid and wide-eyed in the presence of such indifferent beauty, stealthy as a soldier slinking toward her, so close now that he can smell the hot mist of her. He can read the word and allows it audibility in the form of a question: "Luminary?" And she, accustomed now to this inquiry from strangers, prepares to expound on the word's meaning as she turns and sees him.

And sees him. What a thought.

And then? Oh, and then. Happily ever after, you know that. It makes a nice story, doesn't it?

TWO

FEW PEOPLE KNEW THIS, but my mother was given to dancing fits in the kitchen.

She'd be there making her unrivalled cabbage soup, the bone-white fringe of her ancient house cloak trailing the terra cotta tiles that had absorbed a generation's worth of oil and lemon and broth, when suddenly the angels or devils that lived inside her would move her to dance. Hers was no ordinary dance, none that could be classified as jitterbug or tango or waltz. No, she danced like a wild witch over a cauldron in a darkened wood, only she was not destructive. My mother simply had a constant need to celebrate her life.

In the afternoons I would bounce off the school bus and into the kitchen to find her making soup for that night's dinner. I was so little then that I could not see what was going on even if I was standing on my toes, so my mother would let me sit on the countertop beside the cutting board. The black pepper would be hovering over the pot in a Belgian lace pattern she saw in a museum. The lace circled around my head and unraveled into a fine thread that drowned into the thick soup.

"Salt next, Mama?"

"Mmmm," she would say, concentrating on stirring.

23

"Small fistful."

I wriggled to the sink, washed and dried my hands, scooped the sea salt out of its canister with my bare hand and tried to make an arc of salt leap from my palm to the pot. The salt remained a motionless crystalline heap. The Pulling was not a trait she passed down.

"Baby, just dump it in," said Mama.

Mom who kissed me and left a fat smear of bright red lipstick on my cheek, who wore delicious rosy perfume and smiled across the world. Do I remember her? The dancing, the whirling colors of her dresses, a line from a story we must have invented together, fall away into haziness and the constructions of my imagination. She would not live to know the gift she gave me. The cancer would take her away from me before she saw that her daughter too was a conjurer.

My school was an old peach castle on the water. Outside there was thick crabgrass where we were supposed to play, but sometimes I got bored with counting the spots on the ladybugs that landed on my fingers. We weren't allowed to go near the shoreline, but we did. There were jellyfish on the beach like big opal polka dots. We took turns going to the water and back, trying not to get stung.

But sitting in the classroom later that day, I was able to turn the teacher's words into white noise and concentrate on imagining myself at the shore. I could run back and forth from one edge of the beach to the other, and I had to go to the nurse because my foot burned with the pain of poison. My father was furious with the school because I had been allowed to play on the dangerous sand, but he applied a cold compress and some ointment to the wound no one could see.

The day my father brought me home from the hospital, he held me in front of the bathroom mirror and taught me two things. First, that he was my daddy. Second, how to count to five. Years later, when I felt alone, I would count slowly to five. And that is why I am unsure whether my body became my body inside my mother or whether, like Athena, I sprang full-grown from my father's head. I used to think so. Once upon a time, I split my father's alarmingly intelligent head open like a nectarine and leapt unafraid into light. My mother's body carried me—that much I knew from books—but my imaginative life began not when I exited my mother's body but when I entered my father's mind. It was on that day, when he held me small and unblinking up to the mirror, that I truly came into being. The bathroom walls were yellow and he was a young and shaggy scientist then. He was my daddy, and he wanted me to know it.

He used to give me logic puzzles, take me on walks, teach me about how rocks form and why vinegar froths when mixed with baking soda, sit with me in his big chair, play guitar while I sang "The Lion Sleeps Tonight." He would protect me from the evils he did not know yet, from the hurt that he knew must have begun to germinate even then. He understood the internal violence that would be my mother's family's bequest, but he saw something else in me then, something that came only from him. And while my mother's family was communicative, if dangerously so, my father's brooded. Perhaps, as he held me and speculated on how I would develop, my father thought that at last someone was sent to challenge the loneliness he had come to accept as part of him.

"Mommy and Daddy are in love, Mommy and Daddy are in love."

This was a childhood song I invented, singing the line over and over as I stirred up some imaginary stew in the backyard. As an adult, trying to think about it objectively, I wondered how that union was possible. A man of science wedded to a sorceress. He knew exactly what proportions of chemicals would create a desired result; she listened to the world and Pulled herself into harmony with it. Did he secretly believe in her magic? In a way, yes. He loved her so intensely that he thought he was seeing things when he observed her. Later he became fond of telling me stories of what he thought he saw and attempting scientific explanations for them. He only believed in one kind of Pulling, that which Pulled him to her. After she died, he found his love letters to her in one of her drawers and kept them with a few old photographs in her soup pot.

At that time, the human genome was within the vague possibilities postulated by bad science fiction movies, DNA was a relatively new molecule, and my father's processes for purifying water were novel and undervalued. But in spite of his squelched efforts he loved the sciences and I sensed his pride when I showed him my good grades in biology and chemistry. When I went to MIT he was thrilled, and when I moved to Washington, DC to take a position as a genetics counselor at the big hospital he was satisfied, although he wanted me to be a research scientist with my own flourishing lab. In many ways he was a child exploring the mysterious contours of a chemistry set, and he was happy I joined the institution.

Look at Me

And so, I made a career of extracting chromosomes from fetal cells and analyzing the DNA and discussing with young scrubbed couples how to handle emergent difficulties. And I wondered what my own chromosomes looked like. If I had not been so squeamish about having blood drawn I might have pricked myself and found out, but I was able to resist the urge, not wanting to confront the realities embedded in each of my billions of cells. And if karyotyping had been possible when my mother was pregnant with me? Surely she would have wanted to know whether I would be born with a propensity to the depression and cancer that killed her mother, then her. And what would my father have looked for? In vain he would have scoured the genetic layout for my loneliness. On the photographic plate he would have seen not forty-six bulgy X-shaped hunks of nucleic acid, but a dark girl, sad-eyed like her mother, serious like her father. On inspection he might have discovered—or maybe sensed—that I would be born with red hair, an oddity for a Jew and certainly for his family. But would he have seen the loneliness? The sexual vagaries? The fear?

Gradually he helped me to cultivate my intellect. He was familiar with rage and willing to hazard mine. My father handled my loneliness the way a postman handles an envelope; it did not belong to him, he separated himself from whatever lay below its surface, but he would take good care of it until it reached an extrinsic destination. In the meantime, my memories crystallized. Or maybe I'm wrong: maybe these too are my creation. Maybe, as I've been told, I really was pulled from my mother's body. Maybe I really did go to the museum and the zoo, take violin lessons, run around the backyard, develop breasts and intelligence and loneliness. Or maybe I have no memories. I have only impressions, watercolors of what I think might be the past, huge murals of translucent, bleeding color. Perhaps, as a little girl, my imagination gave birth to a day of blueberry picking and swimming in a cold lake with a friend I wished I had. At the time, the story might have been simple fodder for make-believe games, but make-believe is a strange magic. Those details of our laughter, the round blueberries rolling and bursting on our tongues, the feeling of paralysis as our young skinny bodies hit water so clear you could see all the supple underwater life at the bottom. I built these stories so completely and wanted them so badly that in time the scene became a memory, one I remember as real. I have no memories because I cannot differentiate between what happened and what I made myself believe.

A photograph documents that once, on a bright spring day, I bent over and smilingly sniffed a peony, my little curly head the same size as the flower's exploded globe. But I do not remember what the peony smells like. I do, however, remember in detail what that blueberry felt like on my tongue at the exact moment it burst, its flavor mingling with the pond water on my lips. And at the point when I begin to wonder if I have any memories at all or if I made them all up, I think that perhaps, while the little curly-headed girl in the picture played violin and skipped around the yard, I was somewhere else, living out a different thread of my life. Perhaps, unlike people who attach themselves like cable cars to one wire, never aware of the infinite directions of time and space, I am able to hop with exceeding lightness and precision from one life-line to another, at times vaguely aware of all my lives. It is an endlessly provocative thought.

On one side of the yard was the castle tree. It had evergreen branches that hung down to make a dome all around the tree. It also had branches that were huge enough for people to sit on. I played queen of the forest nymphs inside the castle. I also played superhero with the tree as my fortress, because the tree protected me from everything, and no one could see me.

On the other side was the bee tree. The bee tree had lovely red flowers that looked like trumpets and smelled like a fairy's perfume, but I could never approach because bees made honey out of it. Don't go near it! Don't touch!

Once under the castle tree my neighbor Alex and his friend Jason stuck their hands down my underwear. They were sixteen. I was twelve. I couldn't say don't come near me. I couldn't say don't touch. They were bigger, and I had no swarm of bees surrounding me that would protect me and sting them when they came close.

Sickening, you think? How could two boys who were obviously old enough to know better do such a thing to a young girl? But I was the one to invite them in, testing for the first time my kitteny meowing-for-more-milk voice, soft, derisive, certain, with a mock-timidity that would work unfailingly. I unbuttoned and unzipped my pants and pulled out the elastic of my panties so they could touch. In this moment was my first experience of the erotic.

Or perhaps that came late that night in the lamp-lit

solitude of my bedroom, when I wrote out the details of what had happened. In the sticky cave of my blankets my hands grew weak trying to write each letter, and my face flushed with the shame of my own arousal. I had my first orgasm that night, my left hand manipulating my clitoris while my right hand still tried to write the words without the aid of vision.

With the passage of time it became clear that writing was not enough. I had learned to do it because unchecked imagining was too injurious. Shadows of sadness, scrawled out in too-neat handwriting on wide-ruled pages, my poems were mere excuses to shove something in someone's face, even if that something had nothing to do with me. I tried so hard to please others with these poems, and their comments would please me, however fleetingly. I was not athletic or beautiful but yes, I could write.

But the writing was not good enough to attract others into my world for very long and I had to celebrate my visited worlds alone. I developed an undulating way of moving that spoke an invitation. And so, for the second time, I exploited a great gift to get the attentions of others. Alex and Jason were the first to be brought into this venture. The castle tree was my workshop, the site of my experiment. Yes, they wanted it. They wanted nothing but to feel me pliant under their hands. I began to think that perhaps I had been wrong to think my mother did not bequeath to me some of her magic gift, because I believed I was Pulling them to me. They would not understand, they would not be with me at the moment of connection when the universe spoke to me with the propulsion of a comet. But. "But," and then I would look up at them with coquettish twelve-year-old eyes and I would have something of what I needed.

Most people had grass yards, but the people across the street had stones. They were rounded, pastel, glittering. Quartz, my father said. I picked one up and held it to my face. It felt much better than a pretty wool coat or a plastic toy. So soft and round and perfect. I stole so many. I only wanted to have something beautiful and smooth in my hands.

THREE

"LUMINARY?"

Damp strands of hair clung to my face when I whipped my head around in search of the smooth, white-chocolate voice. That was the first time Jonas spoke to me.

"Yes."

"Are you a prophet? A teacher? A witch?" With each accusation he comes closer, moving like a nocturnal animal in the dark gut of the airplane. We are somewhere above the Rocky Mountains. I have been stretching my legs, ensuring the health of my circulatory system. Right now all the blood flows to one place.

"Correct, sir, on all three counts." My body writhes a little as I brush past him, moving toward the back attendants' station where I will pretend to be preoccupied with my own thoughts while I wait for him. He remains in the aisle, laughing in whispers with a pair of lovers, clearly on their first trip together because they have been holding hands since takeoff. I am well aware of his eyes on me, never leaving me, not even when he speaks to the others. Everything about him is hard and square— his jawline, his shoulders—except that voice, and his dark eyes. I turn my back, my breathing shallow, and suddenly I am horrified at the thought of being 36,000 feet above the surface of the earth. In my imagination the plane disappears and only this man and I hover in the atmosphere. In his gray suit he is a dot, a pencil speck on blue paper.

When finally he approaches me, commenting on my retreat, I look straight at him and say, "How am I being rude?" And then, smiling, "I don't even know you."

Promptly he saunters closer and stands across from me in the narrow passageway, so close I can inhale him. His skin had the exact smell and color of Darjeeling tea, steeped for one minute in a glass mug and held up to bright sunlight. He could have passed through me like steam. He had that kind of energy, precarious and hot.

Looking directly into me he invited me out for that evening. The couple was taking him to the Chloe to drink, and apparently I had to go with them.

"I told you already," I said after arguing for a while, "I'm tired. I've been at meetings up and down California for a week. Tonight I'm taking a hot shower and going to sleep. What am I saying? I don't need to explain myself to you. You don't even know my name yet."

"Yet. I'm Jonas, and there you go being rude again."

"I'm Dana," and I extended my hand, which he did not shake. "I'm still too tired to go out tonight. I don't even care that it's Saturday night—this is a long trip."

"Tomorrow then."

He was tall enough that I had to look up at him, standing as close to him as I was, blocking the service section of the airplane. We stood like that the whole time, he leaning against the wall, his legs spread slightly, me standing between those legs. We must have looked like newlyweds, because of that posture, and because of the intensity with which we stood eye-locked, breath-locked. He was lean and handsome and almost entirely bald at thirty-six. The gold band on his left ring finger never became a subject of our conversation.

He told me that he would be in DC for two days on business and had decided to come a day early to see some of the city. Since he knew no one there he asked me to show him around. Of course I could not simply accept, so I said something like, "I'll be at Pot and Kettle's at around ten. If you feel like tagging along on my Sunday route, you won't see any monuments but you will get a sense of how the city lives." And I gave him the address.

I started seeping into him even then, water in the basement. I would make stalactites and stalagmites of his foundations.

Pot and Kettle's suffers from multiple personality disorder. All red velvet couches and candelabras full of burning white tapers, the interior of this coffeehouse looked like a hedonist's dream. Young, heavily made-up waitresses brought steaming beverages in black glasses to the usually bespectacled caffeine-addicts sitting alone with their books and mournful gazes or in small tight circles of backs. Outside, on the sidewalk, several green plastic tables and chairs were set up under the awning that bore the establishment's name. People came alone or with their dogs but talked to each other about political scandals or recent Kennedy Center performances or faraway wars.

Choosing an outdoor table, I ordered strong coffee,

same as every other Sunday morning, reading the paper, same as every week, but there was an urgency that morning that did not usually invade my weekly ritual. Look around. I could not get past the first paragraph of any article, even in the Books section. I could not join the news analysis taking place among all the other table-for-ones around me. Look up, look around. Attempting the crossword I wondered why my brain felt like a desiccated sponge, why it wouldn't *work*. Look up. Would he come? If he did, I certainly wouldn't be watching for him. Look down, try to concentrate. Fourteen Across: eleven-letter word meaning *trial*.

"Your coffee will get cold."

"What? I know. I get so absorbed in the puzzle though." Smiling, I glanced a hello at Jonas and continued adding letters to the grid.

"So," he said as he pulled out a chair with a slow serenity that seemed almost dangerous, "What are your plans for today?" Again, that resolute stare.

"Finishing the puzzle. Finishing my coffee. Going to the Eastern Market like I do every Sunday." At Jonas's raised eyebrow I quickly added, "Nothing all that interesting."

But he went with me despite my protests, into the sun-spiced fervor of the Market. We wandered slowly through the narrow maze of pathways, of lemons and cucumbers. Piles of pistachios and baklava glimmering gold with honey. Walls of silver earrings and necklaces heavy with pearl and amethyst. The redolence of dried sage and freshly lacquered furniture. Thickly painted canvases, sold by their artists. Scarves and batik and tapestries in plum purple and sea blue.

Walking a little defensively, I observed the scene of plentiful goods, merchants chattering with each other as if they were not fixated on the rhythms of the crowd and ready at any moment to react. A graying man in dark clothing clears a path for himself, not turning his head or changing his stern expression. Giddy girls are enticed by a persistent jeweler. I bought nothing, interested only in this confluence of sensuality.

When Jonas and I paused to sit on a curb and drink apple cider, I commented on the girls buying rings. "Look at them," I was saying, jealous of their skinny arms and their mouths like bright berries. "They're so scared."

"They look happy to me."

"They're all wearing the same high-heeled sneakers. They're all competing for the attentions of the little brunette in the mint green tee shirt. They probably need approval just to pee."

Jonas raised an eyebrow. "But not you, right?"

I smirked. "You know how most kids—when they're learning to walk—use a chair or the wall to help them up? They take a few steps holding on, and then maybe let go?"

"Okay."

"I had a big beige teddy bear named Mr. Oatmeal. He was probably a few inches taller than I was at nine months old. So, one day I dragged Mr. Oatmeal right to the middle of the living room floor, used him to help me up, let go, and I was on my way." It was a true story, but stock.

"I'll bet you were."

"And I—"

"Haven't stopped yet?" he finished for me.

"Well, I'm here, aren't I?" I said, turning the glass so the few remaining drops of juice would coat the inside.

"If you want to do something and your friends want to go with you, great. If not, you're going anyway, right? You don't like to be controlled? You want to be free to do your own thing?"

"Maybe," I said, feeling the defensiveness like insects in my flesh. "Or maybe I've spent so much time alone that I need it."

"Only child?"

"Yes."

"Both parents work?"

"Exactly. At least, they did then."

"And you were at home by yourself. You did have some friends, though?"

"Yes. No, not really. There were other girls I played with, sometimes, but when we got to an age where they wanted to play sports and board games I still wanted to play dress-up and make-believe."

"Make-believe. What did you make yourself believe?"

That I was not solid but something else, vaporous. That loneliness was not a feeling or a mood but an essential quality of my life. That spiders had it right, building every day because the world mocks our reasoning by ravaging whatever we think is stable.

I was not about to answer Jonas's question.

"I grew up in a white house with black shutters and a yard," I said instead. "The yard had two trees, the castle tree and the bee tree. Is there such thing as a weeping spruce? Because the castle tree was an evergreen that wept. That was my hideout and my fortress and I used to play there a lot. I never approached the bee tree."

"You wanted to," Jonas said. I could not decide whether his smugness was attractive or annoying. "And while you were playing in your yard in the castle tree and avoiding the bee tree, you had no friends? No Huck to your Tom?"

I shook my head.

"Were you lonely?"

"Yes. I don't know. It was okay. My classmates didn't really like me."

"Ah, the poor misunderstood artist as a child, socially rejected and alone."

"Definitely not an artist. Socially rejected and alone, yes."

"Nah, I think you were just mean. That why none of the kids at school liked you. Always stealing their pencils and dismembering their Barbies."

"Actually, it's funny you should say that. When I was in sixth grade I had this weird science teacher who was very particular. We had three-ring binders that contained all of our class notes and handouts, and because absolutely everything was in this one binder the teacher would not let us physically enter the classroom unless we had our binders with us. So there was this one girl everyone hated, Lisa Schmidt."

"Unfortunate last name for a little girl everyone hated," Jonas observed.

"Don't even start on that. Anyway, Lisa was always chosen last for teams at recess. Kids actually got up from a lunch table when she sat down. It was awful, and when I think of the cruelty that girl endured I am impressed by her and wholly disgusted by everyone else."

Lauren Porosoff Mitchell

"Even yourself?" Jonas challenged.

"Let me finish my story. So she was the outcast, but I was the weirdo. I didn't know at the time why I did this, but I stole her science binder and hid it at the bottom of my locker. Everyone thought it was really funny when she 'lost' it and wasn't allowed in science class for a whole week. I guess I did it because I was seeking the favor of my classmates. I mean, I was always chosen second-to-last at recess."

"Hmm. Not exactly the brunette in the green shirt, were you? So, how did it end? The didactic sitcom ending, where your classmates weren't impressed and you realized your wrongdoing was in vain?"

"No, worse. After seeing Lisa crying in the hallway for the fifth day in a row, I turned myself in to the principal. I regretted the whole thing. But when the kids in my class found out—it was such a small school—almost every one of them approached me personally and complimented me on my brilliant plan. Even the cute boys. That was my shining hour, cute boys in my class telling me how great I was for stealing Lisa's binder and making her look stupid."

He was looking into me, now.

"Well anyway," I said, "I guess I do have some friends now, at least at work, but I still like being alone."

"I'm here with you," Jonas said, still staring.

"You are." And I stared right back. We held that look for a moment, and I wondered if I was linked to Jonas, somehow. It was a barely perceptible, unfamiliar feeling—not quite love, not quite duty, not quite destiny—but it *felt* familiar. The fact that I was so comfortable was enough to make me uneasy.

40

"Okay," he said, standing up and inviting me with his hand, "Now that we're all here, let's walk some more." He began leading me toward a table of bracelets and necklaces and said, "You haven't bought anything yet. I'm going to buy you a little necklace."

"I already have a necklace I wear every day," I said, pulling his hand like a restless child tugs at a busy adult, only I was strong enough to spin him toward the indoor food counters.

"Okay."

The interior was dense with the smell of raw meat and flowers and bread, but I was pulling him past all that toward the barrels of olives. "It's tasting time." I was stirring the Kalamatas with their wooden spoon to get the oil-drenched ones at the bottom.

"Yummy," he said, biting into one.

"No, no, no. You have to pop the whole thing into your mouth. I can't stand it when people gnaw around the pit. When you're finished with the fruit you suck on the pit until the flavor is all gone and then some. They're scratchy."

"Okay," he said. "I forgot to tell you I got straight *Cs* in olive school."

"Try another one," I laughed. "This time do it right."

Obedient as a show horse, he slid another Kalamata into his mouth, and by the time he spit out the stone, it was stone-clean.

"Very good."

"I get an *A* for this one," he said, choosing a Manzanilla.

"How do you eat gingermen?" I wanted to know.

"Legs first, then arms. Then nibble the body, then

put the whole head in your mouth and let it melt."

I had thought I was the only one who did not start with the head. "Everyone thinks I'm insane for this," I said. "I eat pie crust-first."

"Me too. The cherries or peaches are too good. You want them to be the last thing you taste."

"Exactly!"

We hovered over the barrels, lingering over the Niçoise, Picholine, Gaeta, until we began to feel guilty for not buying any and went back outside to continue walking.

"Well," he said, an olive pit clicking against his teeth as he spoke, "I think I understand why you like the Market."

I kept looking at him, curious. I had not told why I went every weekend to the Eastern Market, and he had said himself that I had not bought anything. If anything, I had walked through the narrow paths seeming unaffected.

"You like the richness," he said. "You like to have all your senses filled up. You're a reveler. You like to keep something more than the things you can buy. You keep the image."

I was about to express indignation, despite his being right. He had not known me long enough to know that, but he continued before I could say anything, looking straight ahead of him as he walked.

"You like the marketplace activity, the moments of action, like when that older woman's eyes met that little girl's, or when the merchant's sentence trailed off into an almost-question and you wondered whether that couple was going to buy or walk. The people at the market, all of them, the buyers and sellers and watchers, are at that moment of potentiality, right before a line splits itself off and becomes the one visible future."

What could I have said, then? That I knew what he meant? That I knew myself to be unraveling all the time? Should I have told him about the capabilities of my imagining? As a little girl, awed by the mysteries of the great castle by the sea called school but bored by alphabet lessons since I knew how to read, I used to roam the halls and cause trouble. But once I learned to journey I did not miss the carpeted corner in the library or the ladybugs in the tall grasses or the jellyfish on the shore because I learned to recreate them, to combine and expand what I had learned. It was not as good as twirling in the sunlight—I was a sparkler, spinning till I was a bright circle, red and blue flames dancing off my body and igniting the field like a firework—yet it was better because I could go to unseen places in space-time. As a magical being who could be in two places at once, or three, or unlimited, I began to see that wandering was more than going from hallway to hallway or planet to planet.

As an embryo (God knows how many cells I was made of then), I traveled to Spain, hearing the quick beat of a pulsing language beyond my mother's heart. The faint music, the rumbling digestion of paella, but I could not taste the saffron. And then—what?—did I kick her? With my father's hands on her spherical belly, I wanted to see their universe through eyes, not yet brown, staring only at my barely-formed feet that kept her awake during her siesta in the smolder of a day close to the equator.

"Are you a reveler as well?" I asked Jonas coolly.

Jonas eyed me for a moment before speaking. "Well, do you want to hear a story?"

More vigorously, "Yes."

He breathed deeply. "My uncle's friend Bill Taxin owned a vineyard near San Francisco, where I live. On weekends my uncle used to take me out there. A few months after I finished my doctorate, old Taxin died and left the vineyard to his daughters, but they had no interest in keeping the property up. When my uncle told me the land was for sale, I gave him all the money I had and sold off some stock and we bought it together. It was winter, and when I went to close the deal I took a look at the land and I could hardly imagine those pathetic twists in the frozen earth would ever bear fruit. Still I smiled at Taxin's daughter and produced my checkbook from the deep pocket of my coat. I was imagining the bright clusters, the sweet crushed grapes, the parchment wine label that would bear my signature."

"I guess that answers my question," I said. "I guess one reveler can see it in another, especially someone as perceptive as you." I smiled at him, but he did not smile back. He was entangled in his story, living it.

"There was another reason. A few months earlier I had spent one night with a beautiful woman whose eyes were the color of tourmaline crystal and whose smile was slightly sinister. She admired the tattoo on my right shoulder blade." Pulling up his thin shirt, he exposed to me two seabirds, wings over water, negative space within a black wave about to crash on the surface of his burnished body.

"She told me a story that night. Long ago, there was a people who worshipped the turtle as a bearer of longevity and a communicator with the spiritual world. When a man caught a turtle, he inscribed his name and the date on the turtle's shell, and tales grew up of men who found turtles five hundred or a thousand years old and wrote their own names, adding to this spiritual legacy. Once, a man found a turtle whose shell was unusual, since it bore not a name but a message: 'Whoever finds this turtle should sleep beneath the nearest tree, and when he awakens he will meet the one whose destiny is fused with his.' But the man was a farmer, and the only people who lived within a day's walk were his six brothers who farmed the fields with him. Exhausted with loneliness, he dragged himself to the nearest tree and slept, and in his dream he fell in love with a woman made of light who told him he could stay with her, but only by letting go. When two of his brothers found his lifeless body late that night, a flock of doves flew from the branches of the tree in an explosion of white light."

We both breathed before he continued.

"Looking over my newly acquired fields I thought perhaps, one day, I would know which tree to sleep under. But this is a fiction. I did buy the vineyard, but out of a need to create and a love for wine. At first I wanted to go to her, to bring her a bottle of my wine, even though one night, one morning were too faint a crossing of our paths to warrant the beginning of a correspondence. She never came, and I never saw her again. This was long ago, or perhaps it has not happened yet. In expanded space-time it is hard to tell, and our senses have only been attuned to one line cutting a path through it like a jungle road. Space-time is dense and wide with enough room for everything many times over, and it is hard to trust anyone, including myself."

"It *is* hard to trust yourself sometimes," was all I said.

"Do you trust me?" he asked, smirking. Without waiting for me to answer, he looked at his watch and changed his tone. "Come on, I want to show you something."

"Not until you tell me what it is."

"Okay, I—"

"Wait! You'll ruin the surprise. Let's go."

FOUR

ON THE NORTHBOUND BUS I suppressed the urge to ask questions. By way of a hint Jonas produced a set of keys from his pocket and jingled it in front of me. Irritated, I swatted it away.

"Tell me more about the weird science teacher you mentioned before, the one with the three-ring binders," he said, diverting my attention.

"Ha, Robyn Spector-Spector. She was so intent on keeping her maiden identity that even when sheer chance had her falling in love with a man with her exact last name, she hyphenated. She drove a convertible—dark racing green, before dark racing green was fashionable—with plates that said 'Robs.' "

"Cute."

"I liked her class, though. Science has always appealed to me. We did an experiment where we cut planarians in half and watched them regenerate. If you cut it halfway down it'll grow two heads—you can imagine the possibilities. Pretty sick. But I liked the microscope. It felt right in my hands from the first day we learned how to use them. I liked the idea of coarse and fine focus. And the way the different lenses felt as they clicked into place."

"Yes. I could see that." He was grinning, but I ignored this.

"Once we looked at onion cells under the microscope," I continued. "We had a section in our binders where we were supposed to sketch what we saw and record our observations. I remember writing down the five required sentences to describe what floated in a circle of bright light. One of my sentences was, 'It was pretty,' and when I got the assignment back I found that Ms. Spector-Spector had written 'OPINION' next to that sentence in accusing red letters. Other than that one-worded criticism, my paper was full of checks, and there was even an 'excellent' referring to the drawing of the cells I had copied meticulously from the slide."

"You must have done well in science," he said, seeming interested. Usually they didn't pay much attention until their dicks were in my cunt. Usually the stories were lures. The ones I told in bars I practically had memorized. Now I was on a bus to an unknown destination in Maryland, using new language to tell stories to this hard-angled stranger who gave a shit.

My father knew I had few girlfriends. He must have sensed how dangerous it would be when I started getting the attentions of boys, and he refused to let me date when I became interested. When I was fourteen I borrowed his small sailboat and stowed a boy away until we were safely beyond the sight of the docks. That was the way I introduced myself to sex, on the rocking water, staining the pale blue of my favorite dress. Later when I became more daring, I would sneak out to my father's tool shed that had served as my secret hiding place as a young girl to spread my legs for boys. I was at a party once in high school, wearing a short dress and knowing how good I looked. I wagged my ass all over the room until the best looking boy took notice. He approached me, slid his hand under my skirt and asked me was there anything he could do to make my night more interesting. I said his hand better not be making any promises the rest of him couldn't keep. We were on the floor of the tool shed twenty minutes later.

I didn't know how to handle myself in relationships once I was no longer the one in control. I got desperately clingy, constantly afraid they would leave me. I tested them. I asked their approval for everything, sickened at the thought that I might do something wrong and they would go away. It was this behavior that drove them away every time, and knowing that changed nothing. It was easier to be the manipulator. It was easier to challenge them to a battle of wits knowing I would win every time, easier to dress up cute and feed them lines and entice them into bed and forget them the next morning. Easier to be shamelessly cruel to the rare ones who tried to contact me later. There was one who noticed the poems in my printer tray and sent me a book of Alexander Pope's collected work. I laughed and gave the book to my doorman.

But the worst, the sickest act of all, was writing it all down. I never bothered learning anything about their personalities because I got to make them up the next morning over pancakes, basing their temperaments and lifestyles on the ways they made love. Slow and he became a carpenter, domineering and he was an overeager junior executive at an investment bank. Kinky and he was a liberal academic or a conservative lawyer. They could suffer from losing a footrace or ignoring a pipe leak or choosing the wrong lover. Always from loneliness. All I kept from my real-life lover were the simplest of his traits—the flatness of his fingernails or the scar that broke his eyebrow—and perhaps a comment on the rare occasion he said something profound or witty. Describing the encounter, reorganizing so I would hate him more, I could invent myself to be wilier, sexier, more treacherous. Occasionally I would write letters to a character as if I was enamored with him. Stolid love was the easiest of modes. In this way I was exploiting every one of them for my own daily pleasure, far beyond the simple coital act.

The act was the slightest pleasure of all. I grew nauseated thinking of it: fucking, fucking, all the time, the hot empty breath of them expelled like slag onto my impassive body. It would be much more interesting, I thought, to love someone, much more of a challenging composition.

"Oh, yes," I was saying absently in response to Jonas's inquiry. "I loved the sciences. I still love the sciences—I work at the hospital doing genetic analysis and counseling."

When I told him where I worked he said, "Gordon Fowler teaches there. He wrote the textbook we used in one of my college courses."

"Professor Fowler? His office is on my floor."

"I met him once at a lecture he gave on new technologies in star measurement. He's a genius, you know, but kind of a freak."

"Really?" I smiled roguishly, sensing gossip for the office. "How so? Is he a *mad* scientist? We're all a little crazy, you know. It's not just a myth."

"Actually, mad scientist mythology takes many different forms, but Fowler doesn't lend himself to any of the categories. He's a special kind of strange. He delivered his lecture as if it were a poem. He seemed a little drunk, although I guess that's not such an anomaly. I don't know—I can't really pinpoint it. He was wearing a fedora."

"Sounds like he's my type."

"Bit of a crush, little schoolgirl?"

"Please. You know, I've never even met him. The academics tend to keep away from us."

"Still," he said, still grinning, "If you're working alongside the likes of Gordon Fowler, you certainly must have done well in the sciences at some point."

"But even when I was small and most of my knowledge of science came from nature walks and kitchen experiments with my father, I loved to learn all I could from him."

"My dad used to show me things too," Jonas said. "I remember he taught me why, when you draw colored dots on a piece of paper and dip the end in water, the colors separate."

"Exactly! I remember when my father taught me why mushrooms grow in the deep woods. But there was a difference—then I could also say, 'Daddy, look at the beautiful trees!' and we would both look up to see the leaves gleaming and fluttering like a living green glass roof. Then I would look down and kick up some soil and just inhale."

"A reveler even then." That eyebrow.

"Right," I allowed. "A few years after those walks, when I was sitting at that lab bench in my science classroom that smelled of ammonia, how could I *not* react to the onion cells? Their pattern was like shining antique lace and their nuclei stood out like gemstones. It affected me. There it is. Opinion. I guess that's why I have such a detached view of my work."

"Well, there was your mistake. It sounds like you listened a little too closely to Robyn Spector-Spector nee Spector."

"That's good," I laughed, but despite my smile I was careful to give Jonas a forceful look.

At that moment Jonas rose and said we were approaching our stop. I had not been paying much attention to our surroundings, but I had noticed that the buildings and lights grew ever sparser as we rode. When the bus pulled away it left us alone in the vast night.

"Don't worry, I've been here before," he said gently, offering his arm.

"I'll be happier when we get to where we're going."

"Going? We're here. When was the last time you saw this many stars in the same sky?"

I looked up.

"Follow my hand," he said, sweeping an arc across the full expanse of sky. "You'll notice that all the planets tend to stay close to the ecliptic, the plane containing the Sun's apparent orbit around the Earth."

"I wouldn't know a planet from a star from here."

"Some of the stars you see were so far away that by the time their light travels to where we can see it, the stars are extinct. I had a professor once who said it was

like looking into the past, and that that was the clos-
est thing to time travel we would experience."

"It's an odd thought, isn't it? Seeing something that
no longer exists." He didn't answer, so I kept staring up
at the light-freckled sky. I felt silly, outmatched. "I
know a few constellations," I finally said. "That one is
Orion," I said, pointing. "Although I guess everyone
knows that."

"Orion is my favorite too. See the big bright orange
star at his right shoulder?"

"Where? Okay. Is that Betelgeuse?"

"Very good."

"Lucky guess."

"Betelgeuse is a supergiant. Many thousands of times
the size of our sun, but on its way out. You know, the
bigger they come."

"So what happens to it? It explodes?"

"Actually, it implodes because of gravity. Sometime
in the next few million years, our boy will collapse on
himself and explode outward in a supernova."

"So I was right," I said with mock pride.

"Sort of."

"Tell me more about Orion." Now I was trying to be
alluring.

"The bright, bluish-white one at his left foot is Rigel."

"Pleasure to make your acquaintance, Rigel."

"Rigel's just a baby. But the best part of Orion is the
second point in his knife—the Orion Nebula. Or M42, if
you prefer."

"I prefer the word *nebula*—I like the way it feels.
The Orion Nebula looks fuzzy," I said, squinting. Then,

turning to him, "So, how do you know so much about this?"

"I am an astronomer," Jonas said, still looking up. "That's why I'm in DC—to submit a grant proposal."

"You never told me that! I just assumed your vineyard—well, I guess I should have known as soon as you said you went to a lecture on star-measuring technology. I'm sorry I didn't ask sooner. That's really fascinating."

"Well I, like you, grew up loving science, but I allowed myself to get passionate about it."

"You did say something about a doctorate. So, what are you working on?"

"Mostly I study supernovae and the formation of elements inside them. Rare elements, anything heavier than iron, created in the snarl of exploding stars."

"You make it sound pretty wonderful, but I couldn't see doing that every day if it was something I treasured that much. I think I would get so wrapped up in what equals the integral of what that I'd never go stargazing."

"What are we doing right now? Why do you think I became an astronomer? Do you think all I do is measure parallaxes and write equations?"

"Maybe I would if I knew what a parallax was."

"I never had a teacher who told me I was not allowed to think it's pretty. I do the proofs, sure, because I have to make some money and because I actually enjoy the physics, but the night sky with her stories—she was my first true love."

"Maybe I'm jealous. I mean, I like my work and I care about helping the couples make decisions they feel happy about, but even the vortex machine isn't this exciting."

"Well, come on," he said, indicating a rise just ahead of us.

"Where are we going? To the top of that hill? It can't possibly be any clearer from there."

Jonas laughed as we started walking, and in a few moments I knew why. The hill was not a hill but an observatory. Jonas walked into what seemed to be a deeper black than the night's, but he knew exactly where he was going as he unlocked the outer door to the tunnel that led in. I followed him up a narrow spiral staircase with only sound to guide me until we were in the dome. The red light was disorienting. While I tried not to stumble and disturb the magnificent telescope at the circle's center Jonas was focusing and tinkering with the lenses, all the while explaining precisely what he was doing. I wasn't listening. I knew from the bars that red light was an aphrodisiac and wondered briefly if Jonas brought me to the observatory for that reason. But no, I let myself believe. He was not trying to impress me or seduce me, not directly. He simply wanted me to experience this place.

"You're lucky to get this view," he was saying. "You can see some of the shadowed parts."

He took my hand to help me up the brittle stepladder so I could peer through the telescope at a perfect crescent moon, a shape a child would draw, the whitest silver I had ever seen. So bright it burned into my vision, but I kept on staring without a word until Jonas touched my shoulder. I almost jumped before regaining enough control to look at him, and when I did a purple crescent of afterimage halved his face. Crescent. Crescendo.

"Let me find something else," he said, pulling a

switch that sent the whole dome revolving. If the whir-ring sound had not accompanied it I would have thought I was imagining it, the spinning. Blinking hard I surren-dered the ladder to him.

"Oh, you're going to love this. . . ."

"So let's see it." Letting Jonas's hand rest on my back, I looked at the sphere hovering in the large black field of view, bright and surrounded by a few tiny dots of light. And the rings, wide and bright.

"Saturn," I murmured.

"Those little points around her are her moons. You should see four."

Four moons and a cold planet. She "should see," he said.

"Do you want to see the Orion Nebula? I mean, I got it sort of in focus," Jonas said. I was thinking, not about Saturn, but about the muscles standing out in his neck.

While I was adjusting my eyes he said, "You see the clouds of gas? At her center, you'll have to take my word for it, are four baby stars, the Trapezium, that—"

"This is unreal," I interrupted. A cloud in constant flux, throbbing with color.

He put his hands on me and ran them lightly from my shoulders down the length of my arms and held me by the hips.

"What?" Tilting my head down, I had to wait for my eyes to readjust as I looked directly at him. Firmly I slid my left hand from where I had been holding it at the pulse point in my throat, between my breasts and down my body's line of symmetry, catching the fingers of his right hand and pressing them hard between my legs. He brought his left hand up to my face and I kissed his palm, sure he could feel me soaking through my clothes and "I can't."

"Because—" he started.

"No, not because anything!" I turned to face him. "You think you can take me out into the middle of nowhere and show me some stars and you want me suddenly to go to bed with you? What can you possibly offer me? You'll be gone in a day! You . . . I mean . . . I could have—"

"Dana," he stopped me, "You can wake up tomorrow thinking about what you *could* have, or you can wake up tomorrow thinking about what you *did* have."

I yielded more to the sound of the words than their meaning. Jonas. Could that voice trap my fears like insects in pine tar, petrify them? Fixed, observable, ambered fears that suck no more blood. Dead fear invaded now by light. Could he do it? Even like that, immobilized, the powerlessness is temporary. When he leaves (and he will) the amber will melt and the fears will escape in a wash of pestilence like the Third Plague. So, okay, it won't work, but still I want him here. Get me through this night with lies and we'll worry about the truth in the morning. Isn't that the way it always works?

His skin smelled like spices, like the ocean, and like something lighter, maybe wind. I knew what he would feel like inside me even before he was. We made love so slowly, breathing slowly, levitating over the observatory roof. Like a volcano he altered my landscape, burning the impression of his nimble body into mine in a meteoric flashflood of pure heat.

They both knew they would not be able to sleep that

night since it was so hot, and so they went back to her apartment and lay awake on her Irish linen sheets, drunk on smooth skin and pale light. She did not know what he was to her or, more accurately, why he was anything at all. But there he was, his image, and the powerful suggestion that a sodden and unlit region of him was empty of something only she could give. She could not help but think that if circumstances had been different it would have been more than his body she would allow into her.

Instead, they talked one night until it was day. They told each other stories. He finished his work in her city and returned to his own and she was content. On clear nights like that one her thoughts would return to him, more faithful to the idea of him than she had ever been to any lover.

Did she plan to see him again? Would he differ from the others? She wrapped the sheets around her and walked him to the door. And in the final erotic gesture to transpire between them, she ran her white hand over the tattoo on his shoulder blade. Wings over water. And she let him go.

FIVE

SOMEWHERE IN EVERY STORY there lies a buried diamond. Mine I keep in a dresser drawer, a solitaire that had belonged to my mother, given to me on my twenty-third birthday by my father, worn that day then locked away like the precious thing it was. Something about the brilliance of the morning, I think, makes me seek it, something about the particular way the sun comes in as if uninterrupted by window glass or even atmosphere. The diamond flings beads of light across the wall and dresser and my own pale, bare skin, still sweat-salty from the night before. Beads of light like a broken necklace. Like a disco ball's pattern, spinning as I turn the diamond in my hand and notice the colors. When I tilt it slowly enough I see them all—orange yellow green blue indigo but because of the angles of light and vision I cannot see red or violet. Colors so pure and compact I have to squint to see them, spreading puddles of light.

This morning, unwrapped from the white sheets, here I am, cycling colors. The membranes of my organs pulling taut, capillaries unraveling like a knot.

Do you see that, Jonas? Does that pure and compact light reach you?

I have stolen from him, looted his wallet like a pickpocket, but it was not his money I was interested in having.

On my dresser I arrange my treasures: a business card, a store receipt, the stub of his boarding pass from San Francisco to DC. On the back of the boarding pass are printed the words, "Please retain this stub as evidence of your journey."

Yes. Because years, even weeks from now, there will be no proof. The cells that drank in matter from his body will have died, replaced by other cells containing other words, other foods, other people. These sheets will be washed of his fluids. I will be wearing different clothes, using different shampoo, fucking different men.

"Evidence of your journey." Once upon a time, I loved a man momentarily. We stood in a narrow hallway. We dined on olives and apple cider. He told me a story and showed me a planet. I brought him to my house of wood and linen. His arms made a circle for my waist. I was caught in the circle of his body. Momentary, yes, but I cycled colors. Therein lies my evidence.

His ticket was deemed round-trip, but now his trip with me is only half-taken. He has been gone eight hours, forty-one minutes. How long will it be before he completes the roundness of his trip? Will he knock on my door or will I leave it open? Will he hoist up my skirt and fuck me hungrily or kiss me for a long time, unwrapping my body layer by layer? When he falls asleep will I lie in bed with him or will I be too restless and go into the other room and feign writing? Will I remember to buy syrup for the pancakes?

And when finally we get dressed I will take him to another of my places, Sullivan Fields. It will be raspberry season. The little translucent berries like gatherings of garnet will gleam among the thorns. Dangerous to pick, we will bloody our hands either way—true blood from the dizzying prickle-whirl of green, or that false blood, the sweet kind that will remain on our greedy little fingers from the red crush of fruit.

I will remember that day like breath on my neck. I remember it already like the ghost-breath of a dream. When he noticed that I am a reveler he did not know that I feel possibilities as compellingly as perceptions.

If I am light are you scattered with beads? Do I leave the cycling colors of me wherever I go? Does the light dig its nails into your back? Do you like that?

At work I was in a daily stupor that no amount of coffee would remedy. Vaguely I was following the movements of a couple coming into my office for analysis of their baby's genetic material. They wanted to know what imperfections to expect once the tiny thing emerged from the wife's round belly. Scrutinizing the chromosomes, I discovered that their child would be born with a thrombophilia mild enough that I rarely tested for it but potentially dangerous because of this family's history. She—for I knew the fetus to be female—had a relatively high chance of developing dangerous blood clots in her legs or eyes or brain.

"My little girl!" cried the father-to-be. His youthful face was creased with worry.

The mother stroked the swell of her belly. "We'll keep your blood healthy," she said in a small voice. "And we'll protect you." Then, to me, prouder and louder, "Will there be adverse consequences to her—um—will she be able to have children?"

"Will she even live long enough?" asked the dad.

Lauren Porosoff Mitchell

"There is no associated decline in life expectancy,"
I said, "And of course she'll be able to have lots of
healthy children. Don't worry."

The mother breathed out a few more questions before
her husband touched her gently and escorted her from
my office. What I did not tell them was that the condition with which their daughter would be born would put
her at high risk of developing clots during her pregnan-
cies that could compromise her babies and herself. "Don't
worry." It was a revolting breach of professional ethics
to give such false hope for something that was a statis-
tical near-impossibility.

That night, squinting through the city smog, I tried
to make out a few stars. Where was Orion? I tried to find
his belt but the sky in summer was too orange with haze
for me to see any tiny lights except for signal flashes on
airplanes coming into National.

I needed to get out. Aside from work, I had not left
the apartment in the weeks since the observatory. My
desk was dusty, my bed perpetually unmade, my laundry
like a wall-clinging lichen in the corner of my bedroom,
and every time I tried so much as to put on my shoes I
felt an overwhelming feeling of physical exhaustion. I
had to fuck someone soon, feel like myself again.

On my way to the only straight bar on Seventeenth
Street I stopped at the corner store to buy cigarettes,
asking for my change all in quarters and resolving to
wash my clothes the next night as I patted the heavy
pocket of my thin jacket. At the bar I drank one beer
while watching an Oriole game through the wavy lines of
the elevated television, unmotivated by that night's

round-up of hooting drunks. Thinking that a walk would soothe me, I left the bar and was halfway to Georgetown before remembering Iain and Sepia. Perhaps it was time to buy some new books, but after crossing the bridge into Georgetown and looking for bookstores, the only one I found was one of those large chain stores smelling of commercial coffee drinks and with stark over-bright lighting reminiscent of a morgue. Inside I began to examine the store's offerings of fiction and men and possibility.

In the rigid heat of a night-crowded bookstore, she sheds her jacket to expose her shoulders and breasts, coyly curving toward the man. From her pocket comes a heavy sleet of the quarters she had been saving for laundry, falling to the austere wooden floor in a clatter of disapproval. And look how the lights, meant to promote reading and buying, make them shine. Laundry money? Signal flashes? Stars?

In her pleated skirt she has to curtsey to the strangers in order to pick up her change, smiling in mock-shyness through feet and "excuse me" and sympathetic down-turned smiles, searching for silver disks quiet as uninhabited planets. One of the crazy men is there tonight with his pig-trough hair and pig-skin hands. She glances at his mismatched gloves and leans on a stack of historical novels with a stare blank as new paper.

Her body, blank as a stare.

She makes eyes at another man (probably gay, but look at that neck!) who is looking for new poets. "Sorry," she says, picking up the quarter beside his leather shoe.

If I am lucky I'll remember it that way, as if I was

appearing foolish and strangely beautiful at once, quiet and innocent as the petals of a sea anemone who stings only for the sake of survival. I was more of a lamprey that night, sinuous and slippery and poised to suck the life out of my prey, but even that description is too self-gratifying. I was merely myself, my usual desperate messy-headed self, using my usual finger-flag and back-arch to attract my usual type. This one, thick sandy hair and crooked teeth and a tiny scar on his lower lip from when he split it in a childhood bicycling accident. On the way back to my apartment I commented that only two stars were visible and hoped out loud that one night Saturn would come out. He told me those stationary points of pale color were Mars and Venus, and that I would not be able to see Saturn from the city. Looking at him again, I decided we would fuck doggie-style so I would not have to see those teeth when he opened his mouth to moan.

There is a kind of surreal sensitivity that occurs only when you wake up in the dark. First, inevitably diurnal animal that you are, you resist rising. You shift like a continent on the pillow of earth and remind yourself that you have time for more sleep, but your body is light, and with no string to hold it to the ground it rises like a helium balloon, like a soul, from the bed.

Yes, like a soul, because at that hour most of the city is still in its world of dreams and floats above the buildings in the dark. Perhaps that is why you hear the birds so clearly—not because this is their singing hour, not because there are fewer cars and buses and chatter-calls, but because the acoustics are favorable in air thick with souls. The city slopes up and away from you. Sweat from the previous night has evaporated, so when you rise you are smooth as sea glass.

In the dark I left him sleeping, led as if by an invisible string, body pliant. It was when I was standing by the open window, stretching to increase the surface area of my skin, that I felt it—an encrypted message from far away. In the succulent violet-blooming light came that brief moment of ecstatic comprehension.

So you see, it was not the scream that woke me.

I was in the night-lit kitchen, feeling the air on my exposed body when I heard it, then the breaking glass and the next scream.

Crooked-Teeth comes into the kitchen, his boxers thank God concealing his flaccid penis, and asks if I heard.

"Heard? Don't you hear it now?"

And when he shuts up we both hear the man in the alley behind my building. He is weeping, softly, but I can make out his words. "Please help me."

"Help him," I whisper.

"No one will, you know," says Crooked-Teeth. "Diffusion of social responsibility."

"What?"

"You know, no one helps because everyone thinks someone else will," he says, but the "else will" is barely audible through the approaching sirens. I am grabbing a tank top and jeans from off the floor and running barefoot down the stairwell before he has a chance to ask me if I will be cold. By the time I get to the street, the ambulance must have been speeding toward the hospital for a while because all I hear is the receding siren.

That is when I notice the cold in my limbs, but it is not until after I go back inside and leave blood-prints shaped like a foot in a neat line bisecting the entryway that I realize a shard of the bottle used as a weapon against the screamer had injured me as well.

"Can you go home now?" I ask Crooked-Teeth coldly and without explanation when I get back to my apartment. After he obeys and kisses my numb shoulder I sit down on the kitchen floor and spread open my cut, trying to widen it enough to need stitches. I could watch late-night trash on the waiting area television until a nurse came to dress my wound, but when she left me in the examination room I would sneak around until I found the other victim of the broken bottle. He would be asleep, and I would hold his hand for a minute, then go. I am still wearing my night-chilled clothes. All I would have to do would be call a cab and find my shoes and jacket, but no, no, I do not even know where the ambulance took him.

Slumped like a vagrant against the refrigerator door, my last thought as I was falling asleep was that not knowing exactly where the ambulance was headed was my only reason for not following it.

I woke up with the taste of red wine in my mouth. The sun had just risen and a pristine light fell over the roofs of the city. As I threw my pillows on the floor in an effort to make my bed I noticed that Crooked-Teeth had left his belt, and I enjoyed the sound of the long leather strip slapping the metal sides of the garbage chute.

SIX

"LAST NIGHT IN THE COMPANY of Venus and Mars," I began later that morning, but the pen felt foreign in my hand that early in the day. I was used to the yielding computer keys, and in my stiff fingers the pen's friction against the rough expensive paper seemed too much of an effort. "In the soul-crammed purple night I sensed your message, felt your body like a sentinel making its rounds through mine." When I came to the period and my hand brought down the heavy and purposeful pen, my energy was snuffed out with the sentence.

Watching as ink exploded the period into a supernova, I wondered if a fortuitous move to San Francisco would make possible an affair with Jonas. I could meet him after work at a pub. We could sit on the same side of a booth in an abandoned corner, drinking vodka tonics and talking in double entendres and sliding closer to each other until he flops his head into my neck in mock-drunkenness and inhales the iron heat of my body. I would say I had no money for a cab home and he would say he would drive me but he would need to get sober first. The bar would be closing, but conveniently his office would be close by. He would show me through the maze of empty cubicles to a conference room where we'd sip water from the same oversized cup and talk idly until one of us decided to quit resisting, and we'd make love on the cool polished wood of the conference room table. It would be like that most nights, until his wife would call him and we'd hear the phone ringing through the empty hum of the florescent lights and our own quiet gasps. I would have to compose myself, brushing damp hair out of my eyes, and he would cool off and smooth his suit. His wife would pick him up, and I would exit through the back stairs.

The thought was too much for me, depleted as I was.

Pushing pen and paper out of the way, I let my head descend to the table, one consequence of being too lazy to make coffee. My father once commented on the coffee paradox, how making coffee is the sort of act that requires the physical coordination only coffee could summon. He wished to have coffee elves to separate the paper filters and measure the grinds and pour the water into the machine without splashing all over the counter. I laughed at this sudden memory of my scientist dad, his penchant for nomenclature, his occasional whimsy.

Was I a scientist too? Drowsily I thought about going back to sleep but I had to go to work that day. I was determined to learn more about the stars, and I knew just who to ask.

In sans serif, authoritative typeface, the letters on his door plaque spelled "Gordon Fowler, Professor of Physics."

How would he react to me? Nervous in front of his door, I considered how to approach him. The demure voice, perhaps? "Um, hi. I'm Dana. I . . . do . . . genetic counseling down the hall?" I could stammer. "I was wondering if I could ask you a favor?" I was so nervous I

began to feel lightheaded, but my loose fist was already
knocking on his door.

"En-*ter*!"

I obeyed.

"Oh," he said, relaxing his tone, "I thought you were
my research assistant. He's late. You, your timing is perfect. How can I help you?"

He was serene and attentive as I was at the night-
clubs, and he looked straight into me. Aware of my
breathing, I took quick stock of the office. It smelled of
books, and a clutter of papers and graphs and models all
but buried the professor. Behind him was a stack of
records, one of which played on a classic Victrola that
had a space cleared for it on his shelves.

"Rigoletto?"

"Very good."

"I've heard your music before, but it always seemed
to come from everywhere. Like it was inside the walls
themselves. I'm glad I found its source." I was flirting
with him. I could not help it—I was attracted to the wis-
dom in his turquoise-blue eyes and the messiness of his
office and his slender, angular frame like a praying man-
tis, or like Iain.

"Music is the same as astronomy. My parents were
both music teachers. I still have all of their instruments
in my attic. When they played together, they were describing the way the universe worked."

"I wish I could have an intelligent conversation about
music," I said.

"You can. Listen more."

That was when I noticed the butterflies. Hundreds of
them, stainless steel filigree, hanging at various lengths

from thin wires attached to the ceiling. Something rose inside me, overwhelming me with the feeling that I had come to a place I was supposed to see.

For a moment I looked at the professor as I would an oracle, before saying, "Anyway, I came to ask you about constellations." I was standing so rigid, my hands bolted to my sides to keep myself from fidgeting.

As if acutely aware of my nervousness, he motioned casually to a chair, inviting me to sit down as he said, "What about them?"

"I've . . . well . . . I never took any astronomy courses in college, but lately I've developed an interest in the night sky."

"As you should," he winked. I went taut at this, extending my aroused breasts toward him.

"I was hoping you could tell me where to get more information."

"Try the library." When I blushed he said, "I'm joking. I could give you plenty of good titles, so maybe you'd better be more specific."

More specific? Okay, Mr. Good-Looking Professor, I want to know more about the stars and planets so I can compose gorgeous metaphors in my letters to a hard-jawed, smooth-skinned, white-chocolate-voiced married man with whom I shared one day and night of emotional and sexual pleasure and who lives thousands of miles away. I want to be the woman he yearns for most, and to be her I need to know more about the cosmos, so can you help me please? Please?

Instead I said, "Just something basic about the constellations. What a first-year astronomy major would want to know when she looks through her telescope." I was staring up at the butterflies. There was something about them that I found alluring, something about the way they seemed almost migratory.

"You want a book with maps and explanations. To make sense of the poetry."

"Exactly!" If I had not completely lost my cool before, I did then.

"Well," he said, pulling out a pencil and a pad of blue paper, "I suggest a book called *Legends in Light*. I think you'll find the read informative."

I thanked him, and as he gave me the blue sheet I savored the roughness of his skin. On the paper the title of the book was scribbled in typical professor-scratch.

"Please feel free to come back if you have any questions or further requests. I'm always happy to see intellectual interest."

"Thanks again." But before retreating I said, "You know, I love those butterflies."

"Thank you. I caught you looking up at them."

The following morning I arrived late, and suspended from the window frame in my office were three stainless steel filigree butterflies.

Once, a few years ago, Jonas had another affair, maybe with that woman for whom he bought the vineyard. His wife learned of this brief transgression and forced him to re-earn the sacred marital trust by monitoring him closely. She sometimes crept into his office to see if any odd mail came to him there. And now, though he awaited my letters with fervor, he would not be able to receive them for fear that his wife would learn of it somehow.

Maybe the woman in the vineyard *is* his wife. Maybe she did return to him, as he wanted so badly. Or maybe I am that woman. Should I go to him?

But no, the stories never end the way we predict them. He married someone who he must love a lot, denying himself the pleasure of the danger-eyed woman, and since indulging himself in the physical pleasure of my body he has sickened with the effort to please his wife who sleeps restfully at night thinking her husband loves her more now than ever. And I fuck strangers, and my beautiful clear-eyed angel of the city's innards sleeps alone.

SEVEN

THE BOOKSTORE WAS DARK and tightly coiled and cavernous, the inside of some paper animal's intestine, or maybe a particularly scholarly alien's spaceship. The shelves were not in neat rows like in most bookstores but were placed in what first appeared a haphazard fashion, at odd angles and curves around the room. Iain later explained that the placement of the shelves was designed to lead the interested reader through the store, from one curiosity to another. One looking at Fiction might have the startling experience of spiraling into History. Gardening led serenely into Philosophy, and Poetry, through a strategically placed semi-cylindrical set of shelves, led into War, which led back into Poetry. The unsuspecting visitor was forced through a tangled path of interest and emotion, exploding breathless from the other side with an armload of various books and no time to read them all. At least the well-marked, well-lit rows of conventional bookstores offered the reader a choice. If you came for Fiction, you could get your Fiction and escape unscathed by the tentacles of Science.

"Is there something I can show you?" says the man as he floats toward me. We are two bubbles in the bright room. "I'm Iain," he says.

73

Iain was a violin, lean and hard and majestic, inherently perfect and emanating discord only when seized by the wrong hands. Iain even looked like a violin, slender and sleek as polished wood, his eyes blue and hopeful as music. I watched him then as a scientist watches a scorpion: determined, afraid, but aware of an advantage.

"I am—I thought you could help me find a book on constellations. *Legends in Light*, it's called."

Wordlessly he begins moving toward a corner of the store. Does he know who I am? No, there is no tension about him as he streams through the knot of books, looking over his shoulder to be sure I am following. It is dark enough that he would not be certain, or does he simply not remember? Did Jo ever give him the letter?

He pulls a volume from one of the shelves, slides his hand over the glossy cover and hands the book to me. Turning the pages I see photographs of stars and planets and nebulae and other bodies. The book contains various cultures' interpretations of the skies, how they used them as legends and spirits and oracles.

"Forgive me," he is saying, "but I would have predicted that one for you. You look like you would be more interested in the stories than the science. Dana, I think?"

"You know who I am!" I wanted it to come out more coolly than that. It didn't. I would learn that with Iain I had no power to restrain emotion.

"I liked your note," Iain says. "I was waiting for my life to be a little more . . . orderly . . . before I called you, but I *was* going to call you."

"How did you remember who I am?"

He looks at me, his eyes water-clear, water-bright in

the dark room. "Why wouldn't I?"

"Because we only talked for a few minutes. I'm an idiot." I felt like an idiot. The curious simpleton who does not understand social boundaries. I should not have come to the store. I should have waited until he was ready. But I was impatient.

"Don't ever say that. I remember thinking you could have been the smartest person I'd ever met."

I tried to recollect what we might have talked about that would give him that impression, but all I could think of was his angelic skin. I wanted to ask him what he meant.

"Well," I said instead, "Are you happy I came here?"

"My God, yes. I was only waiting because I wanted to come to you whole."

In a short, nervous spasm of laughter I asked, "Are you broken?"

Georgetown at night is garish and synthetic as a pink rhinestone. They sat by the river and watched over-dressed lovers sip whiskey sours and groups of thin businesspeople having parties on docked speedboats. They tried to go to a back street jazz club but there was a twenty-dollar cover charge neither of them wanted to pay, so they sat on a stoop in the Dixieland-jazz-suffused alley and shared a cigarette. He found a dirt-encrusted mirror and said it had been used as a surface for cutting cocaine.

At midnight he had to meet his friend to sell jewelry at a club. She told the bouncer she was allergic to ink, not wanting to have her hand stamped for fear of liquid acid. She got dehydrated and dizzy and panicky watching the drugged teenagers in elephant-legged jeans smiling and snaking like cherry licorice cords dangling from a mouth. He escorted her out of the club and gave her cab fare. She gave him her building key and told him she would leave her apartment door unlocked. He wrote her apartment number on his pack of cigarettes. She went home, guzzled about a liter of water, and took a long shower to warm herself and rinse away the cloying smell of the smoke machine at the club. When the shakes started she got under two blankets and still it took her more than an hour to stop shivering, relax her muscles and fall asleep. The boy never came.

Dressed up in a cute black dress and mangling super-high heels, I left for the Eastern Market the next day and found him sitting at one of the splintered picnic tables. Laved in pear juice, sucking at the core, Iain said, "God, are you gorgeous."

"Are you sorry?" I teased, raising a curious eyebrow and standing up straight so he could admire my body.

"For what?"

"Last night, you asshole. You were supposed to come over."

"I know. Adam was smoking all my cigarettes and he threw out the pack. I was going to call you but you never gave me your number."

"I absolutely did," I protested. "In the note I gave to Jo." My voice had dulled to a whine that I tried to suppress. Iain's excuse was bullshit—I could see that much in the thick web of arteries across his eyes—but I wanted to let it go.

"Well, I came here just so you could find me."

"Yes, I suppose I do know how to find you when I

want you," I winked.

"Let's go watch soccer," he said, standing up. "Scotland is playing Spain."

With his hand on the small of my back, he took me to the basement cigar lounge of some bar on Pennsylvania Avenue, ordered a brandy for himself and a big soda for me and sat me down on a blue velvet upholstered loveseat from which we watched the whole game. Afterwards he wanted to take me back to his apartment, "to ravage you," he said. He must have meant "ravish."

"Iain," I began.

"I'm just kidding!" he defended. "I'll take you out for the best dinner you can imagine, okay? I just want to stuff you with chocolate ice cream and fill your arms with flowers." But first we had to go back to his apartment so he could change out of his thin and threadbare cotton clothing.

It was cool and still outside, and in the faltering light as we stepped in and out of the row of hazy orange circles cast by the streetlights I could barely see. Everything took on a supernatural, too-sharp quality like the bubble-full figures in a cartoon. Where was I? Was this car really so smooth and red? Could I truly see every sparklingly rough surface of every stone in every house? I was losing my breath. Was this air really air? It could not possibly be because it was so clear. In that difficult light the images were in such sharp focus that I thought there must have been nothing between myself and them, that there was no air, that I was truly in an empty space. As we approached Iain's house I brushed against him to be sure he was alive. As if understanding, he took my hand and pressed it to the pulse in his neck as he led me up the path.

"I should warn you, though," he breathed, before opening the door. "A pipe burst a few days ago, and the place is a mess. I've been trying to get everything dried out." And we went in.

I looked around at the destroyed rooms. His living room consisted of a large marble-topped desk, couches and chairs, and a tastefully mirrored bar with mostly unopened bottles. Had it been a normal day, the room would have been decorated with cheap antique candelabras and family photographs and glass vases. Instead, the guts of his life lay displayed on every flat surface like an open cadaver. I was up to my knees in it in some places, rolls of film and stacks of photographic paper and chemicals and piles of lenses. Field notes lay smeared and damp in front of a heating vent, and three fans blew the whole lot into a lavish confusion.

Across the hall, in his bedroom, a huge plastic sheet was duct-taped to the whole floor, and the massive wheezing ogre of a dehumidifier in the corner spouted hot air, inflating the sheet and giving the room the look of a dark moon. What interplanetary will brought me here to these smells of wood-rot and heat? What monster was that, crouching in the dark?

We never got out of that thick-aired apartment that day.

"What was the story with that guy you were meeting the night I saw you on the metro?"

"Oh, Garrett? I guess he was my boyfriend, sort of. I fell for him for his complexion—creamy and untouchable as polished teakwood. He had a five-star education he liked to show off by talking all the time, but I learned to tune him out because he liked dance concerts and mussels and tying me up. He was a corporate counselor so he always had to leave early in the morning. I had a dream once about some graduate student, Randall, who used to run experiments in the drosophila lab at work. We were at a party, in my dream, sitting on the floor in a big circle with some people I don't remember. Suddenly Randall, in this dream, just unzipped and out comes his dick, only it was forked, and there were a couple of other little ones sprouting near the base and a long skinny one like a worm with no head. And this five-penised monster was wriggling like Medusa. I just started blowing him, like I suck everyone, licking the head. Or I guess heads. Now that I think of it, I woke up next to Garrett sweaty and hot, and I mounted his morning erection and rode it until I came."

"Dana, not to sound insensitive, but why are you telling me all this?"

"Because, after I had that dream, I stayed late at work one night and seduced this Randall, just to see if he really had the deformed penis. Of course, he only had the one, but that didn't stop me from fucking him. When Garrett ate me out that night I wondered if he could taste the latex. He never said anything about it."

"Do you still see Garrett?"

"I haven't in a while."

"Do you want to?"

"No."

Was I warning Iain or myself?

He begged me to allow him to take my photograph. And although I explained that I was shy about having my image preserved I said I would do it, thinking perhaps this boy with his lucent eyes and lucent soul might be able to see me, even through the camera lens. He brought me to the basement of the townhouse, where he had to rearrange the light table that he had brought upstairs because of the flood. Before I undressed he was thorough in showing me the harsh light and the soft, the backgrounds in white and black and wavy-line and checkerboard, the various thin fabrics he would use to drape my body.

I got out of my clothes as easily as I would alone in my bathroom before taking a shower, no slow seduction or passionate rush. My lips were still stained red from the night before. My father, as soon as he saw me newborn, said I had kissable lips. And there I was, pale and red-lipped, with old eyes. No matter how much I sleep I have a pair of blue half-moons framing my eyes, a familial relic from my mother's side.

I was about to untwist my red hair so it would fall wildly around my shoulders when he said, "Leave your neck bare."

She is nervous in climbing onto the table, feeling the weight of the act. The room is cool and damp, not yet recovered from the wrath of water. The first photos would be simple. He directs her to lie on her back and tells her he would take several frontal shots, varying light and background. She lies back and closes her eyes to the bright light and stretches up, her breasts feeling the kinetic energy of the air, her nipples exposed to the hot lights. The camera does not click but she can hear the film advancing.

After he changes the background, she crawls back

onto the table.

"Hold that," he says. "I like the way your shoulders look in this position. Let me just change the light." She is supine, her head on her fists, her arms bent out at thirty-degree angles, her shoulders arched up and her legs bent and spread wide. The hot pulse of the lights tricks her; an illusion of motion makes her think he is approaching. She feels the blood of her blood reaching out, the bones of her bones threatening to come through her skin so they might touch him. His body is torturously close.

"Sit up," he says, and begins arranging her legs to take the light. Steps back, scrutinizes. "I'm going to put my arms in the frame, to make the shot more interesting." His arms and her arms are coiled around her legs. Holding the bulb of the camera in his mouth, he uses his teeth to execute the shot.

Iain and I have cherries and popcorn and root beer for dinner. He tells me he had not responded to my letter because he was recovering from a drug spree. Do I really want to bring a recovering cocaine addict into my life, open the doors of my protected sanctum to this squandered and confused and frightened creature? I feel too much hesitation. I should end this soon before it hurts me badly. But what is it about my life that makes me less lonely or scared or vulnerable or broken than he is? What about my body is less wasted, sexual glutton that I am? I brought him into my life on purpose. Being with Iain makes me dizzy, as if I am entering a drug den myself. His presence holds that kind of surreal, timeless quality, that heat and pressure.

"I'm in love with you," he says, and I know he isn't lying.

Then, giggling, he tells me he knows I am a slut, and not because of the story I told him. He knows because, he says, I have an unusually large clitoris. He knows also by the shape of my body. People who have bodies shaped like mine are aroused all the time and they have abnormal amounts of sex, often with many partners.

"It's okay, you can't help it," he says.

This infuriates me. I look at his vile grinning face, put on my clothes and go.

"WHAT?" comes his bored and guiltless voice from behind me.

I was jealous of the other girls but I refused to be one of them. I did not read series fiction; I did not have legs so skinny that if you blurred your vision they would disappear; I ate all of my cookies at lunch instead of making a big production of throwing them away. I wrote poems and stories and letters I knew I would not send. Sometimes I read books about pairs of girls who got in trouble together. The conflict varied somewhat—one would get her period first or move to a different town, or one would start to do something dangerous like drink alcohol or have sex—but in the end, the friendship between the two girls would prevail somehow. In my writing I mocked the girls at school who had this kind of manufactured closeness, but in my reading, tired-eyed and expressionless with the bedroom door shut, I would learn the lives of these fictional girls who understood each other. None of the real ones wanted to try to understand each other, or at least not me. They would ask each other, "Come with me to the bathroom?" And I would say, "I'll go!" But they would pretend not to hear me until someone else offered to go, and only if no one did would they suddenly notice my offer.

It became easier for me to be alone than to accept a social life knowing I was last choice. And so, the small groups, the inner and outer circles, the premium on talk and acceptance and interpretation were not my domain. I learned instead how to interpret others as an observer, an outsider watching through my microscope lens as these women spoke a language I had not learned. And the boys? In seventh grade I was not a girl, but I was not a tomboy either. Sports were as insipid to me as fashion magazines.

In ninth grade the boys discovered me back. Further proof that other girls were stupid came when the boys made funny jokes and the girls did not laugh. I would sit at my desk shuddering with the strain of suppressing my laughter. And then, with my short skirts and developing boob-ettes I made them interested enough to follow me home, interested enough to use words like "slut" to describe the mystery they saw when they looked at me. One afternoon a gaggle of them followed me home from school. Behind the house at the back of the large yard was a thick of bushes that went right up to the fence. It was there that one of them, the boldest, the ringleader, put his hands under my shirt, where my little breasts were free, still small enough that I did not have to wear a brassiere every day. It began to rain, and my nipples grew erect at the touch of their cold wet hands that slid in succession under my shirt. Then one of them unbuttoned my jeans and put his hands between my legs.

"It's cold!" I screeched. He grinned and, as if to answer, went down on me with his hot little mouth, doubtless his first taste of female genitalia. There was barely enough hair on my vulva for him to have to pick it out if his teeth. It was the most pleasure I had felt in my life but if I moaned or told them to do it more, they would be offended and stop. They had to think they were "doing" me, that I was there for their pleasure and violation, that I was a slut but did not actually *like* it. Stupid boys. Later, in high school or college, they would figure out that for a man to violate a woman properly, he has to get a blow job till her jaw is sore and her lips are numb or fuck her from behind and pretend she's a hired whore. Then I had to learn new ways to play on their stupidity to get my own pleasure. But there was a brief period when their fascination with the heretofore unsurveyed feminine topography was enough of a draw.

So it was during this period that I led five or six of them into my backyard and had one licking my cunt, one sucking my tits, and the rest looking on in incredulity. Then one of the peepers warned us that a lady was crossing the backyard.

It was Mollie, the woman who came once a week to dust my father's books and make the beds, coming to find me for dinner, looking absurd as she shivered and shrunk under her tiny umbrella and crossed the spongy grass in her house slippers.

"Dana! Dinnertime! Are you out here? Come in, it's raining!"

"Shhhh," I whispered, then added a "My father will kill me if she tells him you were here." This satisfied the boys enough to shut up and continue, but Mollie kept coming. I warned them to hide but there were so many of them she could see the gaudy colors of their jackets standing out oddly against the dripping green trees. I was about to reach orgasm.

"I'll be inside in a minute!" I screamed through the rain, and my bare feet burrowed and twisted into the mud as I came.

The next day I culled the hostility of a fresh harvest of rumors at school but for months I had different boys eating me out whenever I wanted them. Was I a slut? Was it predestined by my grossly oversized clitoris?

EIGHT

I WANDER HOME FROM IAIN'S in a strange fever. There are days I get dizzy, lightheaded, when I am at once listless and acutely aware of the world. I notice this on my walk home through Dupont Circle. Two men play chess; two others stare as I cross the street. I am aware of every fluttering leaf on every bush as surely as if they were blood cells in my own body. The yellow tulips listen to the wind. It will rain soon.

On days like this, I often look at my hands to remind myself that I am still real. In the hot wake of a truck I hear, "hey sexy" and my hair blows all around me in my fury. Spinning, and the world in over-vibrancy. The shapes are too well-defined to me. Sometimes I am sorry to be wearing my glasses. I would rather view the world through the mysteries of astigmatism, distorted and blurred, than have to face this diamond-cut clarity of late spring. Papery calyxes blow from their former buds and dance in the gathering breeze. Yes, my hands. I am still real.

Is consciousness a stream? More like a jagged mountain. You fall down it and get caught up in places, badly bruised from the shock at times, and at times it is a pure free-fall without awareness. What is this now? What is

87

this city of deep colors and right angles?

At home I go to the sink for water and notice the mound of dishes. A plate pooled with festering tomato sauce. A bowl filled with water and a few sunken grains of rice bloated and pale as drowned bodies. Ring-stained coffee cups and so many teaspoons. I run the hot water to rinse the dishes for the dishwasher, but before I can pick up the wet blue sponge my hands are bearing down on it, gray liquid seeping out, my sobs masked by the slurps of water into the drain. My lungs are collapsing. It is an eye-squeezing, body-convulsing, teeth-gritting cry, stifled even in the privacy of my one-bedroom apartment. And then, the shapes and colors again, image persistent like an over-repeated word that loses its meaning. I begin to say the words out loud. "Dish." "Sink." "Counter." This is a tile floor, this is a table, this is a window, and yes, there is air in here for me to breathe. No, I need to get out. There is the mirror, there is me, reflection of a body made for sex, a woman pushing all the fingers through the thick red hair, nails digging into the scalp, palms touching the pale frightened face. Palms cold on the hot face.

Eyes closed, the horror of the apartment is still with me.

I manage to load the dishes into the machine and curl up beside it. I love the dishwasher. The familiar, non-toxic, reassuringly lemon-scented white grains of soap powder. You can fill up the little cup as sloppily as you want but when you close it, it levels itself off. Then the gentle rumbling, the rhythmic swirl, the low hum of drying and whoosh through the pipes as water floods the dishes again. The warmth of the dishwasher door. Sometimes I sit for the entire cycle on the yellow tile floor of my tiny kitchen, leaning on the washer, knowing order will soon return, if not to my life, then at least to my cupboards. When I open the door I will feel hot moist clean-smelling air on my face, and I will bask in front of the open dishwasher until the drinking glasses are cool enough to touch.

In the early morning, my computer heartens me. Perhaps I can make him real, conjure him through my work. Pinocchio and Galatea pirouette closer. Didn't the gods make us of river clay? Didn't we make our gods from words? If we can make a god, why can't I make a tall, narrow, nearly bald man with skin that smells like Darjeeling tea?

But I have the wrong myth. He must be Eurydice for I am Orpheus, singing so sadly that even the trees weep. When he returns to me, I will follow him into hell, and if I keep myself from looking at him, we will return to light. But no, he is irresistible, and I damn us both.

From the corner of my top dresser drawer I produce the business card I stole from Jonas's wallet. I could send my letters there. I imagine him opening the envelopes, ripping them neatly but eagerly. He will brew a pot of coffee after most of the others have gone. In his office he will have me to himself, spread out on his desk. He'll be stirring his coffee absently as he looks at the words like welts on the page. When he lets me inside him it will be slowly at first, then with increasing speed as his desire mounts. In this way we can make love all night.

You will keep that night inside you: a dewy August, one where a heightened sense of touch allowed us to feel every moist blade of grass. And your heat.

I wonder if you remember my breathing, molecules of air once within the wet crevices of my body hailstorming yours. If you are haunted by the persistence of my language on your neck. But there is more than this. When you read a book do you notice the paper or the words? I have been through your printing press, and the pulp and pith of my body no longer matter, a mere vehicle, inscribed with desire.

I write him letters like this one and keep them under a pile of papers in my bottom desk drawer at work. A dry winter approaches. I pick at my chapped lips, and when I hold my letters to my mouth I leave a print of blood. When the madness prevails they will trace it back to words. I wonder if Jonas would see in the black language the dark sea creatures that sleep here. I wonder if he would know I am one of them, not a warm-bodied woman but a slippery octopus among them, hiding in the purple cloud of my own ink.

As I put away the letter and almost notice the files on my desk, a new thought surfaces. Jonas's wings-over-water tattoo bounds through my head, only in this fleeing image the birds take flight from his back and soar away, multiplying, until there are thousands of them following at each others' wings.

Sometimes she dreamed of Orion, the hunter, the only man ever able to win wild Artemis' wild heart. But they could not be together, not in the way that made Orion ache. He was a hunter, and he would not have known how to love the goddess without holding her. Love could not have existed for him without possession, and she was not to be kept; her only request of her father Zeus was to be able to be free. And so, Artemis and Orion became friends until Orion's passions could be contained no longer. He wanted, just once, to experience his goddess in all her naked glory, to hold this feeling in his mind forever, even if he could only hold her once. For this, Artemis' jealous brother Apollo sent a deadly scorpion after her friend. And now they inhabit the night sky.

And with the last loop of the *Y*, my pen tore through the paper.

The scorpion will never catch Orion. It is doomed to chase him across the ecliptic until his stars burn out, he unbuckles his belt and casts down his sword and the scorpion, exhausted by so many years of pursuit, loses its poison and withers. But for now, and way after we die, the two hang in the sky and we invent stories about them. They exist above us as a constant source of potentiality, a reminder of the moment of action, rather than the act itself. They are at the instant that splits one road into many, but in our story we see only one outcome.

Many outcomes are possible from one event. And instead of developing tunnel vision, of seeing the one that seems to occur, we must develop our outer senses, the sixth and seventh and eighth, that allow us to perceive the divergences that sprout from every event. The scorpion catches Orion and stings him to death. Or: Orion draws his blade, swings around and slays the scorpion, and from its body emerges a beautiful woman trapped for years, waiting for the prophecy of her freedom to come true. She gives Orion the kiss of forgetfulness, and he thinks of Artemis no longer. Or: The hunter and the arthropod grow tired of pursuit, stop to rest, discuss physics for a while and become friends. Or: The scorpion finds a new battle to fight, and Orion sits on a stone and scratches his head in wonder over how he will live now that he has nothing to run from and no one to run to. Or, and Or, and Or. The constellations have excited us for millennia with their prospects, their infinity of stories. And we learn to accept the infinities. For example.

Loneliness is standing on the back porch with no wind to spiral through your hair. You stand in the night's stillness, staring into the neighbors' yard at a white ball reflecting the deepening orange of the sky. Your solitude is contained in the jangle of the chains on their swing set. Your eyes drift back over the fence, past the darkening magenta of azalea bushes, past the heavy curls of a vine, settling on a bird that pauses at the gate, calls to its companion, flies away. The sky deepens, a water glass in which some artist keeps dipping her blue-stained brush. Now everything stagnates in blue, and yellow light glows in every window of the house that stands behind you, even though no one is home.

Or: Freedom is being able to stand patiently and pensively on the back porch, appreciating the azalea bushes in bloom, their last blaze before sunset. A sparrow pauses to sing at the gate. And when the sun finally sets and the planets make their first appearance, you notice the gold light in every window, a reminder that nothing is ever empty.

The sparrows fly off toward the river.

Wings over water.

And I let him go.

NINE

HE KNOCKED ON MY DOOR one Sunday evening, bearing two Pot and Kettle coffees in paper cups, a Walkman, and a mango from the Market. He was so breathlessly exuberant as he thrust a coffee at me that I had to ask if he was high.

"No! I just saw something wonderful!"

"What?"

"Wait. First I have to take your picture."

"What? Iain!"

"*Pleeeeeeease*? I have a few shots left on this roll and I don't want to waste them and I have to develop today."

"On two conditions."

"One?"

"Give me that mango."

"Two?"

"You tell me what the hell happened to you!"

"I will, but first you have to let me take you."

"Let you take me, eh?"

"Your picture!"

"Okay," I said, spreading my arms in I-love-you-THIS-much fashion and smiling goofily. "Take me."

"No, Beautiful. Here, sit on the floor and eat the

93

mango and listen to this," he said, handing me the Walkman. "It's my brother's bossa nova band's demo tape."

Uncertainly I obeyed, and by the time the camera stared to flash I barely noticed it, rapt in the fruit and the music until Iain pulled off the headphones.

"Now are you going to tell me what all this excitement is about?"

"Okay. You know how sometimes there's a mounted park policeman on Dupont Circle?"

"I don't see them too often anymore. Once last summer I stood petting a horse for my whole lunch break. They have big eyes."

"Yeah, well, today I was hanging out at the Circle, sitting on the fountain and waiting for the sun to begin setting over the guys playing chess, and all of a sudden from behind me, I hear this 'Haah! Haah!' and the horse starts galloping down Connecticut Avenue. It went so fast that I only had time to take one shot of the horse's butt and galloping legs and the cop's back leaning down over it like a trained jockey and this little kid walking with his mom, pulling her arm half out of the socket and pointing. I wish I was in better shape—I could have chased them down the street. I can just imagine the rich wives milling around the stores on Connecticut Avenue, seeing this big glossy horse like in a bad Western. There's got to have been shopping bags flying and cars stopping short and people jumping out of the way. I wonder if any reporters saw. They'll probably just interview some of the bystanders, but I got the horse! I hope there's a kicked-up dust cloud in the shot. I can't wait to see how it came out!"

"But you just had to come over here and tell me about it first," I said, grinning, and his smile changed from awe to affection.

"Dana, you were the first thing I thought of. Well, I've got to go develop these," he said, and was gone before I had a chance to say anything. Had I forgiven him? Somehow, with Iain, I was able to delve into the part of me that wasn't angry.

The Eastern seaboard is experiencing an unseasonable November heat. If it were not for the wan light and the yellow leaves that left their acidic imprints on the sidewalks, it could be summer. Iain and I are sitting at Pot and Kettle's drinking our third cup of coffee that morning. Would I have invited any other to partake in this delicious Saturday event? Would I have let any other invade my essential solitude? But he is not really there to me, because I am thinking of nothing. My muscles, despite the huge influx of caffeine and sugar, are flaccid as a patch of moss after rain. I suck slowly on my coffee, hoping it will have some effect. I want to be vibrant and beautiful with Iain, but I am saggy and soggy and empty. My eyes and eyelids struggle.

"Dana? You know what you need?" Iain says after a long silence.

"What, Iain? What do I need?"

"You need an afternoon to play with me. Let's go to that apple-picking place you told me about."

"I can't. It's too late in the year for Sullivan Fields," I grumble, smiling despite myself.

"Whatever. We're going."

Iain grinned triumphantly as I buttoned my sweater.

Lauren Porosoff Mitchell

I stuck my tongue out at him and he laughed. Protests were not an option with Iain. In the welcome simplicity of Sullivan Fields I might have been swallowed, by earth maybe, or by sky. The two of us wandered through rows of late Jonathans.

Iain among the fallen apples. An apple is not like an orange or a banana—it does not fall away into discrete sections. It is whole and polished. Once bruised, it rots. Once cut, it browns. An apple is perfect or else ruined.

"Dana," he said, drooling apple juice, "You're going to find someone amazing who treats you so well, and he'll take you to Sullivan Fields and you'll never go with me anymore."

"Iain, we're going to be eighty years old with kids and grandkids and great-grandkids and we'll still go to Sullivan Fields."

Iain threw his apple core into some tall grass and put his arm around me. "Okay, Dana, but I'll be in the middle of my fourth divorce by then. You're going to find one man who's incredible and will love you forever. As soon as you meet, you'll both know."

"I don't know, Iain. Don't you think sometimes you can meet someone and love him but not get into a relationship?"

"Like me and you?" He winked. "You know, you're right. We don't have to have a relationship; we'll just have good sex."

"Iain!"

He was climbing a tree, a Red Delicious fastened to his mouth. In the late fall sunlight he looked so brilliant, so incorporeal, that I might have been imagining him. Perhaps he would rise from the tree like a dove or a spirit, leaving only an apple core to prove he had been real.

"Iain, are you real?" I had to ask him. He vaulted down from his perch.

"Am I real?" And then, smiling, "No, I'm your dream boy. You'd better not let me pinch you!"

"No, I mean, did I make you up? Tell me about your parents. Tell me something I know I couldn't have made up."

"What do you want to know?" he asked, slackening. "My dad used to be an air force pilot. My mom is a journalist. I'm their greatest disappointment. What else do you need to know?"

"My father entered the military at eighteen," Iain is telling me, both of us large and sprawling with our apples on his hardwood floor that was finally clean after the mess of the flood. "He was dedicated to his service for thirty years, and he didn't meet my mom until he got out."

"Wow. He must be almost eighty by now."

"And he's keeping bees."

"Bees?" I crunch through a mouthful of apple.

"Bees. The kind that sting. The kind that make honey if you're lucky and treat them well. I remember when they tucked me in at night my father's hands would smell like clover and my mother's would smell like lotion and money. I guess it's bizarre but it seems normal to me. You should meet my mom. You'd like her."

"I think I'd like your dad."

"Yeah, too much. If my parents have managed to stay together for twenty-seven years I'm not going to let you be the one to break them up."

Iain's father retired from the service looking young and healthy. He had not married, never having met any women he liked better than his airplanes. Once he retired he was lonely, and at church one Sunday a sharp-witted news magazine writer picked him up and took him home and spent the rest of the day and the night and the following day in his bed. They married, she had babies and he had bees. Eventually she missed her work and left Iain and his two older brothers to boss each other around. When his brothers became interested in sports and girls, Iain's only source of comfort was his Spanish-born grandmother.

"I never knew your grandmother was from Spain."

"Galicia," he says.

"I always assumed with a last name like McArdle and your blue eyes your were a true blood Scotsman."

"Get used to being surprised by me." He grins. I grin too.

Iain's grandmother, or *Abuelita* as he calls her, lived alone in a small apartment building in the Ironbound section of Newark, populated by other immigrant widows. Iain went to visit her often as a small boy to lie on her linoleum floor and eat cheese sandwiches and play canasta at *Abuelita*'s lamplit table. Even as a delinquent teenager, Iain came to her thin and pouty, and feebly she would heat up some soup and tell him stories about the part of Spain where she was raised to be pious and robust.

"Once there was a fire in back of the building," Iain tells me. "The story was that one of the grandchildren was being careless at a barbecue. The saddest part was the burnt flowers." Then he spoke of the charred azaleas crumbled into an ash layer on the back patio, pink to black to dust blown by the slightest breezes from the old women walking with their watering cans. "I guess they wanted to bring those old bushes back to life," he says.

"Wow. No one was hurt?"

"No one. It was a great miracle, *Abuelita* said, especially since there were children around. Everyone got out in time, and the building itself wasn't damaged at all. *Abuelita* said it was my great-grandfather watching over her, preventing any major harm. He was a saint, you know."

I shiver. "A saint?"

"I never told you this story?"

"When would you have?"

"I don't know. I was there when she found out. I was seventeen. *Abuelita* was in her kitchen, wearing her turquoise-and-yellow striped house frock, eating fish soup and drinking club soda with half an orange in it, because that was the only way she could still enjoy oranges without getting acid indigestion. I was scrubbing the stains off the coffee percolator, and the phone rang. Grandma waved a hand at me so I got the phone and it was the Vatican. They somehow got her number. Her father was going to be sainted, and the whole family was invited to Italy for the occasion."

"Did you go?"

"Yeah, we all went. I got to see my Spanish cousins. I'd only met them once, when I was very little. Usually we only went to Scotland to see my dad's family there, because he's practically royalty. I guess it's worth a big reunion when you find out your ancestors are saints and angels."

I knew there was sainthood in his blood. I did not believe in his god, but I believed there was something fighting for air inside his broken body, something no X-ray or karyotype would detect.

"What do you think it's like?" I ask Iain.

"What, sainthood? It sucks. You have to suffer a lot and then be dead for a while."

"No, I mean the afterlife."

He is still for a minute and then says, "Hell is a burning skeleton child sucking at a hot breast that spews mercury. Heaven is full of tiny cloud-blue pairs of hands touching faces of gold."

"Where the hell did you get that?"

"I don't know. Just came to me."

"No, I think it just came to *me*," I say quietly, knowing it is the saint inside Iain speaking just to reassert itself. "I mean," I add quickly, standing up immediately with great unseen effort to throw away my second apple core, "I'm lucky I got to hear that."

"Whatever," he half-laughs.

"No, I—it sounds like a pretty good photographic creation. Maybe that should be your next big project—a tribute to the fates of your great-grandfather and your best friend."

But instead of laughing at the joke, he says, "If I have to die, I want to be stabbed to death in a bathtub."

"What?" I am aghast.

"You know how in the movies," he continues smoothly, as if he is envisioning tonight's dinner and not the violent circumstances of his own death, "Someone gets whacked in the tub, and the water turns red from all the blood? And later the hero finds the poor guy and we see it?"

"Iain, we need to get you some antidepressants. Maybe some ice cream too. I mean, I've had bad days but—"

"Would you do it?"

"Sure. Do you want chocolate or cookies and cream?" Why am I making jokes?

"No, I mean would you stab me to death? Not until I'm really old, of course, but when we're like ninety-eight and our kids and grandkids have long since sent us to a retirement complex in Arizona and I'm about ready to die, I'd love to have it be you who kills me. I could set up the camera ahead of time—maybe you could lie in the tub for me so I can figure out the lighting. Then you knife me a few times, make sure they're in major arteries so I go quickly and the wounds really gush. You wait an hour or so for the blood to diffuse and you photograph me. My old saggy pale skin and blue eyes open in fright against the cherry-red water under soft light. What a stunning visual."

He has been ranting maniacally, breathlessly as I attempt to suppress the apple and acid mixture looming in my throat.

"Iain, do you realize you're talking about your own death?" I ask, my voice solemn this time. "What would make you think about it now, and so violently?"

"Would you rather I die of cancer? Heart disease? At least this way you get the shot."

I try not to imagine it, but I see it anyway: Iain dying into his art in one last indulgent spectacle.

"I'm planning to die in the middle of an erotic dream." In spite of myself I imagine Professor Fowler's music attic, the two of us making love among old cellos and tarnished flutes until my heart gives out in a spasm of ecstasy. The professor would have to be about 150 years old by then. The Hebrew word *zahken*—'old man'—surfaces in my brain. What is it I contain and restrain inside me?

"In the *middle* of the dream? Wouldn't you at least want to finish?" he asks, picking up a core from the table and clicking his front teeth over the last bits of peel near the stem.

"Can we talk about something else?"

"Sure. Speaking of my mastery in the visual arts," he says, wiping his mouth on his sleeve and his hands on his pants, "I want to show you something."

Iain is spreading out his work on the wide floor of his apartment so I can help him select one more shot to add to his final portfolio for school. I look at him, bright and otherworldly, crouched among the photographs like I used to crouch among ladybugs in the tall grass. He chooses for the show with the precision and practicality of a cook choosing zucchini, but to me it seems an excuse for routine sensuality. He too, a reveler.

"What do you think, Honeypot? The mango or the armoire?" he says.

One photograph is of his own armoire, spilling out sweaters and rumpled jeans, the top drawer open to reveal his camera lenses and coin collection and a dried osiana rose his high school girlfriend gave him. Through double exposure, the mirrored inside door shows his misty rippled image reflected in a pond. As a dark grainy silhouette, he manifested himself within the deepest secrets of his room. A self-portrait. One self.

The mango is of me, or at least I recognize the appearance of my body. That is supposed to be me, sitting on the floor of my apartment, leaning forward with my legs bent up, position of a child playing jacks. I am wearing headphones, listening to bossa nova, but my concentration is on the fruit. I had peeled back part of its skin and bit into it whole, the juice glazing my face. Iain tricked the lighting for the viewer to see it, golden in black and white. It was not a photograph of me but of Iain, once again.

"Why not both?" I asked.

"Why not?"

He is lounging now on his barren floor, having put away his photographs. In the darkest of caves lives a species of fish with organs visible through skins like glass. This is Iain now, open to the full bloom of afternoon light. If I were to look a little closer I would be able to see the lacework of his capillaries. When he looks back at me I am sure that if I could pull one eye out of its socket, the sudden beam of light would strike me blind.

Could I know him, then? Could I walk through his inner ruins? The surer I was of his position, the less sure I could be of his velocity. He could be speeding away from me right now. He could jump up and take my picture, or read to me from one of his many books, or bake me a pie, or decide he wants me to leave him forever. Or, and or, and or. The thought was making me sick. But look at him. Look at his vitreous skin, his lithe movements. Surely if this fragile young man did not have divine capabilities, he had something close. He would be the one to know me. There is a photograph he has of me, one of the nudes, where he asked me to place my hand on my stomach and move it away quickly just as he was shooting. The resulting print contained both a ghostly hand and a substantial body. Through his own arrangements of energy Iain was able to see everything at once.

Iain is a photographer. He knows about negative space. He is telling me about cities in Europe, how the rows of houses have such a gentle symmetry that we notice instead the square. Remembering Rome, he says, we remember not Rome but the shape of space around Rome. I have a vision of a fountain in reverse, its air spilling out into the water. We think of the structures, not the un-thing but the thing. And what does it feel like to be the shape of space around me? Who decided I would be solid and not open, figure and not ground? I think these thoughts and they float from me, into the anti-me-shaped air around me. They spin off my spinning body alone like me, into the background set off by my figure. Radiating like heat.

Iain is still spread out on his floor and talking about the shape of space around Piccadilly Circus when I yield to a flush of heat and kiss him, long and deep.

For the second time, I stretch out naked for Iain. This time he has undressed me, kissing every part of my body as he did it, and with every kiss my muscles harden into a tighter cringe. I am trying to relax. Did I leave my favorite pen at the office? Maybe I'll go get it tonight. Maybe I'll pick up some files too so I won't have to read them Monday morning. I think I must have eaten a spoiled apple and my God Iain stop it! With his head between my legs I have to close my eyes and concentrate only on the physical pleasure, yes, no, what pleasure when his tongue feels like a cold fat frog on me? I close my eyes, imagining several of the men I have fucked in the last few months, one at a time, two at a time, anything to try to forget who it is whose mouth is really on me. And then he moves my hand to touch his penis. I am disgusted at the thought. What's wrong with you? You've done this hundreds of times. I grow callous. He tries to enter me, but I can only look away coldly and squeeze my legs together. When he tries to open them it makes me so angry that I dig my nails into his back.

"What the hell was that?" he asks, irritated.

I tell him about my octopus soul.

"You're over-dramatizing," he says, putting on his boxers. "I don't know what your big secret is, but does my little girl really have such big problems?"

I went out that night wearing red silk. I sucked one stranger's cock in the bathroom at a club and went home with another. This second had a copy of James Joyce's *A Portrait of the Artist as a Young Man*. I pulled it off the shelf and said excitedly that the moment of "Stephanomenos! Stephanophoros!" changed my life. He said he was forced to trudge through the book in high school. After he came all over my tits and fell asleep I put his book in my coat pocket and listened to his contented wheezing as I crept out.

Walking home at five in the morning, the world is a different city. After the last desperate drunks have stumbled out into the streets, after the lovers have furtively found their own bedrooms and the traffic lights flash just for show, this is when I am almost at peace. I realize it is unsafe, that any of the rare passing vans could contain a predator, that no one would come to my rescue if I scream, but it is not worry that I feel. Something about the synergy of a hauntingly quiet city and my own exhaustion calms me. I walk quickly—dangers wait with grinning mouths and grabbing hands—but I walk nevertheless, from the prison of interiors into the tranquil night.

It is five in the morning. An inflated plastic grocery bag blows like tumbleweed across my path. A construction worker in dirty jeans and a torn red baseball cap breaks the lull bidding me good morning. A tree is filled with birds like leaves that will rise with the sun and leave the tree bare-branched. One sleeping alley is lit with gas lamps and smells of decaying leaves. At this hour when it is not night and not morning, a scampering and serious world is reduced to images. I am not wearing a watch.

Instead I measure time in my languor. I know that when I return home and look in the mirror, I will see the woman he knows. My eyes red encircled with black, lips swollen, hair a crop of tangled wire after long and unsettled hours. My cheeks pulse with him as they did that night. I lie down in my bed, try to rest, and among slow, sleepy night breathing, the one sharp gasp will be you. The purple light that forms behind my eyelids is you.

When Iain came over the next morning he said he was willing to forget that night ever happened.

"You should be the one apologizing," I said bluntly, about to close the door.

"I'm trying to. Here, I brought you something."

Through the six-inch gap I left in the doorway Iain hands me a fruit.

Look at Me

"An orange? I don't know, Iain, last time it was a mango. You can't fruit me into submission every time."

"It's a blood orange. Have you ever had one? I got up extra early this morning and went to the Eastern Market to look for something for you. This is innocent looking enough, but wait till you peel it. Wait till you taste it. It reminds me of you."

"Thank you, Iain. I'll call you later, okay?"

Into the silver bowl with six other oranges I place Iain's gift and for the first time I notice its red tinge. I will eat it for breakfast tomorrow. The air outside is dense with frozen gray moisture and light barely filters through closed curtains. I spend the rest of the day in awkward suspension between slumber and alertness, unable to awaken fully or to fall asleep again and nothing, not even the peace of a dull day, is accomplished within the frustration.

And now, what would he see? Look at this achy body and swollen face. It is Sunday night already. I have just taken a bath, and I am standing naked in front of the full-length mirror on the back of the bathroom door in my dirty one-bedroom apartment. Eye makeup drips down a red face. I scratch at a mosquito bite on my thigh until it bleeds. Who am I really? I am this, sitting naked and cross-legged in front of the computer by the window that leaks cold air. I am this, steamed and sticky and red-faced and cold, alone at night in a cluttered apartment, at my loneliest and most pathetic when I want to tear my own flesh apart to make it worthy of his.

Look at me, sitting here at nine o'clock on a Sunday, making errors in my typing because of the cigarette between my fingers and ashing all over the worn keys of

107

my laptop. I squint at the four words on the screen. How am I supposed to write when I can't even see? I insist on not wearing my glasses, even when I'm alone and even though I know damn well that it makes my eyes worse. I should not feel empty. I should feel grateful. I should never buy another pack of cigarettes. I should call my father every week. I should focus on my wonderful job. Why does everything have to be so fraught with fear?

I decide to make vegetable soup. Mama's recipe, written in her barely legible handwriting on the back of a tax form, tells me the secrets of her famous dish, and though I know mine will not taste like hers, I long for the huge smell of her to saturate my tiny apartment. In a narcoleptic struggle I put on my sweats and sneakers and find my wallet and head for the supermarket. Outside my building two women appear to be waiting. I recognize one of them as Malia. She has eyes like jet, and I know her name from looking at the addresses on her mail when we come home at the same time. I hear her call her companion Linda, who must be visiting Malia because I've never seen her before. Malia is wearing a long red satin dress, platform shoes and a thin wool coat. Thin lips. Linda has blonde hair, slicks it back like a model's, and wears a black skirt and a gray tailored jacket. She and Linda are going dancing. They are meeting two tall Europeans at the club. The men will buy them long elegant drinks and light their cigarettes for them. Linda will get prissy and bitchy early in the evening, complaining she doesn't like her guy enough and isn't drunk enough to dance. Malia will complacently allow Linda to lead her out of the half-crowded club and back to her apartment. They will make tea, some homoerotic tones will underlie their conversation, and they will sleep in the same bed but not touch.

I go to the supermarket around the corner to buy chicken and tomato and onion and parsley. Walking from aisle to aisle I grow dizzy from the pulsing light and the endless rows of cans. At the sight of the neat pageant of cash registers my inclination is to drop my heavy basket of groceries and run, but run where? Back home? Then I will be wanting the soup again. I place my items two at a time onto the sandy conveyor belt and watch them parade like Noah's animals over the scanner and into plastic bags.

"Okay," I say out loud to the sloppy array of peeled vegetables on the counter, "Who's first?"

Delicately I place the naked whole chicken into a pot of water and watch it steam, then boil. "Wait for the water to play tag with itself," my mother would coach.

She used to say that the act of love takes a long time to develop. Years, she professed. And I know she experienced a level of trust and understanding that I have not, but I like to think that I have loved many, truly, in the deepest sense. "I like to think." What does that mean? "The deepest sense." What bullshit. Love so deep for one that I refuse to send the letters I write, so deep for another that I cannot forgive him a moment of honesty.

"Skim the foam," I repeat my mother's instructions. After a few minutes of scooping up chicken suds I relent and call Iain to invite him over for soup. I hope, as the phone rings for the sixth time, that he is not out freebasing with his druggie friends.

"Hello?" comes his sleepy voice.

"Were you sleeping?"

"No," he says groggily.

"You liar."

"Okay, I might have closed my eyes for a little bit. So, are you speaking to me again without a fruit offering? I think we're making progress."

"Have you eaten?" I ask, trying in vain not to let him hear the grin in my voice.

"Yeah. My upstairs neighbors made steak. Digestion is rough work," he growls through a yawn.

"Oh. Well, I'm making my mom's vegetable soup. Let's see . . . carrots, celery and onion next. Add them whole and then simmer and then purée and *then* add the chopped vegetables? Wow."

"Sounds like a pain in the ass. Why don't you just get a can of something?"

I ignore him, add the celery and carrots, and notice them displacing the broth dangerously close to the rim of the pot.

"You're supposed to put the onion in whole, but it doesn't look like there's room for it," I tell Iain.

"So take out some of the water."

"Well, let's just see." Slowly I lower the shining white sphere of peeled onion into the pot. The soup overflows the pot, and because the chicken fat rose to the top it is the first thing to spew out onto the stove, and what happens to volatile fat when it meets an electric burner?

"Shit, Iain! My kitchen's on fire!"

"What?"

"You know, because of the chicken fat!"

"What?"

"What do I do?"

"I don't know! Throw some water on it?"

"No, it's a grease fire!" I fling open the refrigerator, produce the baking soda, and hurl a wild torrent of the white powder all over the range, the floor, the counter, the soup, myself. I am breathing coarsely, coughing baking soda out of my lungs.

When Iain hears silence he asks, "Did you get it out?"

"Yes. The soup's ruined. Full of baking soda."

"Okay, well, I'm coming over and taking you out for enchiladas."

I am still staring in stupefaction at my powdered kitchen when I hear Iain's knock.

"Let's see the mess," he says, bolting past me toward the kitchen. Still standing in the doorway I hear, "Whoa! Looks like a brick exploded!"

"A brick?"

"Of cocaine, dear. Don't worry, I haven't been doing any. If my eyes are still red it's because *someone* woke me up. Come on. Let's go eat. We'll clean this up later."

As we walk to the Mexican restaurant in the moistly shimmering night I say, "Iain, thanks for coming and hoisting me out of my catastrophe. And I don't just mean the soup."

"Little girl," he says, stopping mid-stride so I have to backtrack to look at him, "I don't know what you think is wrong with you. Look what you've got. You've got me."

He is grinning, big and half-fake like a school kid on class picture day so his blue eyes squint and his dimples are deep as wishing wells.

"Iain? Hug me?"

And he tackles me so we are knotted in a mess on the Seventeenth Street sidewalk, scuffling and sweating and laughing up tears until we both glow.

TEN

I WAS NOT ACCUSTOMED to seeing him look ugly, but he did then. His waxy skin fit his face like a badly-made dress, stretching over his forehead and cheeks but sagging under his enlarged eye sockets and mouth. A thin crust of blood lined his nostrils and mustached his upper lip.

"My God, Iain," I said the wrong way as he fell past me through the door and slumped against my writing desk, almost toppling my computer.

"My God, Eee-yan!" he mocked me.

"Look—"

"Sorry. I get bitchy when I don't eat."

"I'll make you some spaghetti."

"I don't want spaghetti."

"Then what would you like? I'll make you anything you want, as long as I have the ingredients."

"No, I don't want you to have to cook."

"I don't have to," I said, exasperated. "Tell me what happened. What's wrong with you?"

"What's wrong with *you*? I can just *leave*, you know. You don't have to *pity* me."

"Iain. I just meant that I want to cook you some lunch. Let me make you something."

"No, I want to take you out."

"Okay," I said, feeling tired suddenly. "Where do you want to go?"

"Anywhere you want. Not pizza."

"No, I don't want that either. How about enchiladas? On me. I owe you enchiladas anyway. We can go sit outside. It's a nice day."

"I don't feel like Mexican."

"What about one of the other places on Seventeenth?"

"I don't know. Maybe."

"Well, where do you want to go?"

"I don't care! I'm starving!"

"Well, there's bread and leftover chicken in the fridge. Make yourself a sandwich," I said, disintegrating into the couch.

"Fine," he said, not moving.

With a resentful sigh I rolled off the couch and went to the kitchen to make Iain's sandwich. Thrusting it at him I said, "Eat. When you're finished we're going for a walk."

"Fine," he said again.

"You're welcome," I said.

"Thank you, O gracious Chef Dana," he huffed. "Is this left over from the soup disaster?"

"Don't fuck with me, Iain. I know you were snorting that shit last night. I can see it."

"My God, Dana," he said through masticated bread, a tinge of shame in his indignation.

"Iain, don't fuck with me. Now finish that and we're going for a walk."

I sat on the floor next to him and watched him stare

out in front of him and eat the sandwich absently, letting small pieces of bitten chicken fall clumsily to the plate.

"You're right, you know," he said once he finished and set the plate down next to him so he could wipe his face with his hand. "I was bad last night. Really bad." And then, more desperately, "I don't know if I can quit. I'm trying."

"I know you are."

"I am!"

"I know! And I'm going to be here for you."

"Really?"

"Yes." I knew I didn't mean it, that I could stop seeing him and let him waste if I chose, but I wanted him to feel safe with me and respect me and need to be with me.

"Dana, I think you're the sweetest person I've ever met."

The sweetest? He brought both of my hands together in his, holding them tightly, until I told him it was time to go.

It was a warm December and the city was full of birds. You could hear them, resonant as jazz in an alley, the music coming off the pavement like steam. You could see them, splashing in puddles and crowding the trees, leafless in the weak sunlight. You could almost touch them as they hopped clownishly about the sidewalk, delving for crumbs and seeds in the cracks of the brickwork. If you were lucky one would swoop down, cooling you with the breeze of its wings. The sparrows and larks and grackles were everywhere, and singing.

Iain was walking with me through the heat, insisting he was comfortable in his jeans and long-sleeve shirt and windbreaker because the sun was so low in the sky.

"It's almost solstice," he said.

"It's 77 degrees."

"It still smells like winter. Even in the heat."

That exemplified what I loved about Iain. He dressed based not on the temperature report but on the smell.

I said, "It smells like winter, looks like fall and feels like summer," and the bird songs grew louder, as if to agree.

"You forgot spring," he said. "It sounds like spring."

I threw my arms around him, almost tackling him to the ground and startling a woman walking her Norwich terrier. When I let him regain his balance I kept his hand clasped in mine, and as we walked we were swinging our arms in time with the changing rhythms of our conversation.

"I remember one fall when I was little," I was telling Iain, "In Vermont, it sounded like spring because the birds left late. I even asked my dad if they would make it south before the winter came or if they would leave their little W-shaped footprints in the snow all over the yard. He said they'd get out in time. Anyway, the birds were singing and my mother was pregnant—"

"I thought you were an only child."

"I am. She had a miscarriage."

"I'm so sorry."

"It's okay. You know, I never really thought much about it. I was only four when it happened. Mama and Dad kept telling me about the little brother-or-sister I would have, and my mother and I would talk excitedly all the time about whether it would be a boy or a girl

116

and how I would have to hold it to give it a bottle. Then my mother went to the hospital for a long time, and when she came back her big belly was back to normal and she didn't want anyone disturbing her and Dad said I wasn't going to have a brother *or* a sister. I really don't remember giving it much thought after that. I must have been pretty happy being by myself."

"You seem to need your solitude."

"Like you're the first person to tell me *that*. I'm wondering now, though, if the baby was stillborn or if it had a genetic problem."

"That is your specialty, isn't it?"

"I can't believe I didn't think of it before. I look at chromosomes and big bellies every day."

"Do you think *you'll* ever have a big belly?"

A lark in our path finished its business on the sidewalk, fanning us with its wings as it whooshed up to a telephone wire. "I hope so," I said.

"Anyway, tell me about the day with the birds when your mom was pregnant."

"Right." I had to transfer myself from one mental tableau to another. "A painter was doing a circus mural in the new baby's room. I kept going in there to watch the lines and colors turn into monkeys and lions and an elephant and a juggling clown on a unicycle and a ringmaster with a big top hat scaring a bunch of bees and butterflies with his baton."

"Wow."

"Oh, you should have seen it! Mama was in the kitchen baking carrot cake. When it was ready I brought cake and apple juice to the painter and the gardener raking leaves in our yard. I remember that day smelling like nutmeg and paint and leaves and sounding like birds, just like today."

"You had a gardener?"

"Yes."

"We didn't even have a garden," Iain scoffed. "Not when I was younger. Although now my father has a vegetable garden and a flower garden. It's a really weird experience to see your father, who used to be this hard-ass air force pilot, cutting back forsythia and tying tomato plants and weeding the dirt around the peonies."

"We had peonies too," I blared.

"Yeah, and you had a gardener come and manicure your estate," he teased in a bad English accent. "Did you have a butler too?"

"Oh, it wasn't like that at all," I said, giving Iain a playful slap. "Danny went to the University of Vermont and he did yard work in some of the nearby towns to make money for books."

"How quaint."

"I guess. Danny drove a green truck that had a bunch of rakes and other tools attached to the sides, and he kept his lawnmower in the front seat. I used to love watching him load up all the leaves and hurl them into the bed of the truck. He was kind of scrawny-looking, but when he lifted up those massive bundles of leaves his shirt would rise up and all his muscles would flex. He had a great smile too."

Iain posed like a bodybuilder. "Should I be jealous? Wait. You were how old? Four? Isn't that a bit young to be checking out the strapping young gardener?"

"Not for me," I grinned. "What can I say, I was ahead of my time."

"So what happened with the circus room?"

"No one used it. After my mother died my father sold the house, and I think the new owners painted over the mural."

"Are you okay?" Iain asked.

"Yes. Maybe," I said, scrubbing my eye and sneezing. "What's wrong with me, Iain? Of all the things that could upset me from thinking about Mama and our old house, the destruction of the circus parade is what makes me cry."

ELEVEN

AND JONAS?

I continued to invade his body. Soft and furtive, I was the one to enter him. His penetration was hard and loud but mine was silent. He was unlike the others, doleful and diamond-hard with a naked soul, and though his morals were too much for a physical affair I did not want one anyway. I would have wanted to be next to him in the mornings, but I would not have known what to do with him when he awoke stroking me. He would have wanted to make love again and again, shower with me and run soapy hands down the length of my body, smoothing me like icing. And? Would I share my pancakes with him? Would I work in my day-bright apartment with Jonas there in it? He would not have been afraid at the sight of me, naked and calm in front of my computer, sipping coffee and waiting for language to seize me at the throat. Then what? It would have been impossible. I did not want it anyway.

But we did have an affair, and it was illicit, even though it was only through my written and untransmitted dreams.

Dreams? I kept dreaming of Jonas only to awaken alone, blinking away the last images of him and reminding myself that his presence had been weightless.

"Why?" I asked out loud. "I met this man, this stranger who eats pie crust-first and makes wine and tells stories about white doves, and who I'll never see again. Jonas." The mention of his name sent a fresh layer of sweat to bathe my face.

I wrote him another letter.

I think of you this morning, when I split open a blood orange and recognize its red flesh. My skin is so pale—you've seen it in the morning—and the blood orange's blood-red juice drips down my pale hands in the paler morning. And it tastes almost like ecstasy, dark and sweet, but not the honey sweet of an orange orange. Darker and deeper, like my own body, and sweeter like yours, when I'm so close I smell and taste your flesh of firm fruit and your bones of branches.

Blood-red juice runs down my porcelain body and I ache for you.

I want you to be caught up in my branches, my fruit in your mouth. But I am not an orange orange, not so sweet. I am a blood orange, red on the inside, destined to appear to the untrained eye as something I am not. And maybe you will find the juice too sour, too strong, but you are not afraid of peeling me and laying me out open and letting me dissolve slowly in your mouth. I concentrate on that now, because this is one way I can love you in a dark hour, when I have only inventions for company.

In my sprawling hand I wrote and signed the letter. I knew I had to stop writing to him, had to let go. I had done it already, but it was no less difficult for the practice. He was with me. He was in my hand that had been transformed somehow by the experience of touching two birds on his body. My skull had been infiltrated as surely as if it had been trephined.

He had been her lover for one night. She had let him lead her to his magnificent telescope, telling her stories of the planets. He was beautiful, tall and lean with a smile that made her suspect he was always thinking something dangerous.

She knew that their lives were on divergent paths, and that it would have been futile to try to force them together. Instead she lay down on her bed and began to dream a little, and later she could not remember if she had been asleep when she felt his unmistakable presence in her room. She heard a drumming noise at her window and wondered if he had flown back to her astride some great monster of the past, a winged dragon perhaps, that he had encountered in one of the strange worlds he visited. Instead she discovered a white bird with a tiny parchment scroll clasped tightly in its beak and a blue glass vial of coriander tied to its leg. He wanted her to know the scent that infused the air he breathed. The dove, bringing back proof of a distant lover, had touched the numinous winds that separated them and brought the news she ached for. It was a short message, written in black ink that had bled slightly from the humid air, thanking her for allowing him to communicate his passion and asking that she meet him in the middle of the ocean.

This is a true story. If I were inventing it, she would

have gone to meet him at sea. Their boats would have met beneath the Orion Nebula, and the woman's selves would have reunited in another explosion of white light. They would have been happy forever on a boat. But no, she refused his invitation as much as she longed for him, since she knew he was not to be kept, and the only way to have him was to let him wander without her. She knew the paths of their lives were meant to cross and re-cross, but never to run together.

And what did it mean? What strangeness was rattling around so loudly like a marble in a glass, keeping me awake with its reverberations?

Jonas had written me a letter, delivered with a bottle of Trapezium Estates Pinot Noir.

"Dear Dana," his letter began, "My proposal was accepted, and I will have to be in DC at the next full moon. I was hoping to see you, to thank you for letting me communicate my passion to you. You know how to find me."

Find him? I could scarcely find my breathing. Outside was a thin waning crescent. Perhaps he was right. I did know how to find him.

I slid my hands over the wine bottle, luxuriating in the textural difference between glass and parchment. When I read the label to see how the wine was made, I was imagining Jonas lying naked amid his grapes, the sunlight turning his body translucent. It was the phone number printed on the bottle that splintered my thoughts from the warmth of fantasy. I had not noticed it, and as soon as I did I threw the bottle from my hands as if it had turned into an asp. The glass did not break.

I spent those weeks trying not to call him, all the

while planning out what I would say and imagining the various outcomes.

"Jonas, this is Dana. Hi! I can't talk long, but I got your letter, and I'd love to see you. Maybe we could meet for drinks."

Or: "Jonas, hi . . . I'm doing well . . . Listen, it was good to hear from you, but you were right when you said that one night, one morning were too faint a crossing of our paths to warrant the beginning of a correspondence. I hope you'll be able to understand that I can't see you."

Or: "I've been trying to let go, but I've been in love with you since you first looked at me on that San Francisco to Washington airplane and I think we should try."

Ashamed and disgusted, I resolved not to call him. But this too was a fiction—now that I had his number how could I resist?

The heat in my apartment had been on high that late December night, but I shivered with nervous energy. I would call, and we would talk, and the conversation would progress as it wanted to without my conceding too much. I scanned down the bottle for the number, even though its digits were in my memory as certainly as if they had been branded, and with shaky fingers I dialed his phone number. It rang once, several times, but he was not there. Comfort and gloom. I listened to his answering machine message, the poor quality of the tape turning white chocolate into rock candy. After the beep I paused, ready to hang up, but then I blurted my phone number, asking him to call back soon.

He did not call back. I fell asleep every night clutching the cordless phone as a child would a stuffed bear. When I dreamed of him I did not fly, exactly. I was weightless, yes, but I swam through the air. And perhaps those nights I was truly weightless, leaping from one body to another so I could touch him. Perhaps I experienced contact with that other self, the one who did go with him, the one who made love to him in a boat on dark water with a flock of white seabirds wheeling in ecstasy overhead.

It was a particularly clear and bright night in December, the kind of night that felt the way breaking glass sounds. There were six days before his arrival, and I could not sit alone looking pensively at the night sky, watching the growing moon, waiting for it to signal his body. If he came then, what would he have seen? A woman trying to sleep but sitting up in repeating fits of I-can't-breathe, fits of life-clinging panic. A dry woman, a rabid woman wearing white cotton, swaddled in the poultice of a stained white bed, sweat-white and sex-juice-white and venom-white, white as the filth that bath water does not soak off her skin. Endless uninterrupted white, white shades, white walls, white bed. Sanitarium white.

From my dresser drawer I pulled a deck of cards for distraction and my mother's diamond for protection. The window shades flapped like two wings against the glass.

And I let him go, again and again.

Loneliness is being unable to awaken in the pink hour because you stayed up playing endless games of clock solitaire, shuffling hearts and diamonds and staring at the dizzy landscape of paint on the wall. You notice your own breathing and feel suffocated.

Alone and hopelessly grounded in my singular life,

the moon round but invisible in daylight, I feel empty and some part of me catches in my throat. I cough and try to release it, to ease the strain of his absence. It becomes hard, on days like this, to convince myself that I am real. That he is real and once lay in this bed.

Once upon a time my father gave me the pieces of a puzzle and drew various figures that the pieces could fit to form. With cold fingers I worked on one shape for eight nights, and on the ninth he wrote me to say the shape was impossible, that he had been wrong. But I imagined it in my head, that perfect, shimmering shape, and I continued to manipulate the glass pieces hoping for a miracle.

I try to make it work. With desperate energy I imagine a possible confluence at some time in the distant, undeterminable future. The figure assembles itself. I have already written the story of his coming here: the Market, the breathing, the sexual positions. All we need to do is recite our lines. But no, this is the wrong figure, look how that piece juts out where the surface should be smooth, and a frustrated hand waves across the completed puzzle, and the pieces slide across the table. I imagine the shape again, and again I try to build it.

One day I noticed I was holding the piece that matched the shape of the air that remained in the almost-completed puzzle.

But I realize this new figure truly is impossible, and seeing it in my head does not mean it can be formed. I also see in my head the image of my body rising like a ghost above him. Perhaps in one of my lives I soar above the earth with no aid, and the figure is possible, and he

127

sees through to the center of my soul and loves me, because that is all it takes.

But he does not. He does not love me.

And my body broods in agony, angry at itself, feeling for the first time the ripping, wrenching pain of its fission.

His absence torments me, and the thought of his presence upsets my balance.

I have cultivated, here and now and without him, a body and soul that know how to understand the weight of his absence, content to feel him in dreams and dream of him in waking. He could come here, but he would not be the one in my other life. He would be the him that he knows, that he understands, the him that does not love the me that throbs with my own depletion.

But once I had seen the shining figure in my mind I could not let it go.

I consider it more, not weeping, but with the same interest I might have taken in a butterfly's wet wings scintillating for the first time as the new creature emerges from its cocoon. Romantic love was created when it became practical for women and men to experience it. But my love for him has a celestial quality, larger than culture and stretching in infinite directions. It has a windy quality and yet weaves itself into the tangible world. I love him because the world decided I would.

I have been awake all night, and now the sunlight eats the stars like cookie crumbs. In my silver bowl I have a papaya ripening, and this morning slicing it I cut my finger. I let it bleed as I scrape all the black, jewel-like seeds from the fragrant orange flesh, and only when it rests in four perfect quarters do I go to the sink to tend my hand. It is a day fashioned of fate, and if my hand wants to bleed I let it. No, I think, sucking papaya juice. I am taking the portents too seriously.

At that, I run to the phone and tell Iain I am coming over for breakfast. Clutching all of the letters to Jonas, moistening them with the sweat of my palms, I rush to Iain. It will be a difficult morning.

"Dana. I can't believe you never told me any of this," he says when I finish the story in all its fertile detail. I have been pacing his hardwood floor, click-click-click, throughout the telling, and he has been staring round-eyed from the tiny kitchen table. Two plates of cold, syrup-logged pancakes wait impatiently.

"I didn't want the pressure. I thought if I didn't tell you about Jonas, he wasn't really real." My muscles feel like sandbags as I flop into a chair and stare into my orange juice.

"What do you mean? Let's figure this out."

"There's nothing to figure out. He lives in San Francisco. He's married!"

"And he'll be here tonight."

"I have no place for him anymore. If I'd wanted to see him, I would have rushed to California as soon as I got his letter. I would have found him way before that, if I'd wanted to."

"Maybe you weren't ready then. Maybe you are now. Maybe that's why you're telling me."

"Maybe not! Maybe I thought then that I'd built him up too much, built 'it' up too much. Look at this pile," I say, thrusting at him the unsent letters to Jonas I had been hiding. "Sometimes when I wrote these letters, it was like I could recognize my handwriting but it didn't even feel like I was writing them. I think that's because it wasn't really me writing them, and they weren't really for Jonas. I mean, I never sent them, right? I wanted the love affair so badly that I made it up, but it was never really mine."

"Maybe. Or maybe the person who wrote these letters was a woman you weren't ready to see. Like I said, there's a reason you're showing all of this to me now."

"Iain, you don't understand. The dream of him was better than the reality. The reality is some wanderer whose head is literally up in the sky and who spent all his savings on a vineyard because of some chicky he only met once."

"Dana," he says, leafing through the letters, "You know you don't believe that, and you need to forget about this dreaming-is-better crap." He moves toward me, strokes me. "Dana, I adore you and I want you to be happy, so let's figure this out. I don't think turning him into a dream is the answer. It sounds like your feelings for him are not that docile. And you deserve more than a dream. You, you deserve someone you can hold."

"Can I hold someone who holds someone else?"

"I just feel like there has to be a resolution," he says, seeming annoyed but not at me. "Okay, so first I thought, listen to her, these two are Hollywood-style meant-to-be. Then I thought, no, she's right, there's nothing that says love has to mean courtship and boyfriends and multi-tiered cake." Iain rises to refill his orange juice.

"What can I do?"

"You can see him. You can tell him how you feel. You

can give him your letters. Or, you can try to forget him, but at this point do you think you can? Realistically?"

"Or, I can write something else. Something else," I repeat, and Iain looks strange and new.

TWELVE

THERE IS AN ANSWER in simple physics. Newton's Third Law of Motion convinces us that for every person there is an equal and opposite person. We believe in this equation, not simply because generations of romantic experts professed it to be true, but because it is familiar. You place your drinking glass on an end table. You are certain— you'd bet your life on it—that gravity will keep the glass from floating away and that the normal force of the table will keep the glass from sinking into oblivion. Newton's Third Law is faithful and sure. When people whisper to you that gravity theory must be modified to account for quantum theory you tell them they think too hard: if it ain't broke don't fix it. Ah, but if we believe the universe is geo- centric and the trusty old sun still rises every morning, aren't we deceiving ourselves into something dangerous? But this is not the point.

We seek each other thinking there is one equal and opposite person out there. How equal, and how opposite? Someone composes an intimate résumé and seeks someone with similar demarcations, a partner for tennis or danc- ing. A pair meets for drinks, each person wearing a neatly pressed outfit and the buoyancy of health-consciousness, and two glasses of the same single-malt scotch clink with golden-hued satisfaction. Intelligence craves intelligence, beauty fancies beauty. Psychology is proud of itself for confirming such things.

How opposite? The cliché hovers and tempts: opposites attract. My father is a quietly dynamic and brilliant man, a scientist and an explorer, an inventor and a believer. He thinks. He reads. He eats. He sleeps. He builds. He does. He plays. He is. And in each of these endeavors he is large, even in his small and unthreatening frame. My mother was good-natured and generous. She was a net that gave when she caught you, then gingerly yet lovingly released you back to your trapeze artistry. She was a warm, secret place, a hideout filled with goose-down blankets. She saw everything but pretended not to if that was how best to protect you. Her strength still supports and her beauty lines the intricacies of all souls she touched. She is durable. She makes you whole. Even the irritated tone in her voice when she opposed you was a comfort. My mother and father were married fourteen years, equal and opposite, best friends and wildly in love. But this is a coincidence.

The rest of us see this kind of match and assume causation. I love you because you are my equal and opposite reaction. We seek each other thinking one and only one equal and opposite person waits, and those who believe in fate think they are being steered toward that person even now on a path that seems contorted and wrong but actually has laser-beam precision. At birth we lock on target, and the part of life that is not really living is a pre-charted course toward him or her. Sit on deck and get a tan in the meantime. Others, the planners and achievers, believe that finding the equal-and-opposite is an exercise in effort, patience, and self-restraint. Nihilists and skeptics believe that the equal and opposite persons exist but humans lack the requisite luck and skill to find them, and instead we waste in a loneliness intensified by the knowledge that he or she is out there, unseen and untasted. The religious have it easiest; the sought perfection is God, and they strive toward, but do not reach, that asymptotic equality and oppositeness.

And when we find this equal-and-opposite? The glass rests snugly on the table; my parents stay happily in love. What if this equal-and-opposite eludes us? Cynicism or despair, or both. But these negative emotions are only the unfortunate products of our own assumptions, just as the same era that created Newton mandated two-personned love. Perhaps, at least for the daring and the crazy, it is time for an alternative.

What, then? There is another theory that people can never fully meet, that they are parallel lines, aware of each other's presence and prescience but not touching, eyeing each other longingly, aching until the two lines dis-integrate. And in general, I agree with this view. People engage in culturally authorized behaviors we refer to only metaphorically as putting up walls, retreating into shells, hiding. We play games and follow rules, and the ones who refuse are called desperate or deranged or weak. Fear is a luminous and powerful beast.

And yet we long for truth as we play and pretend. I have been guilty of it myself. I kept a scrapbook of silhou-ettes, those of various lovers and friends who have brushed my life and whose best features remain with me. Sometimes I found myself stroking the cover of this book as if to conjure, like a genie from an old lamp, a compos-ite of them all, possessing one's intellect and another's devotion and another's iridescent skin. And like multiply-exposed photographs, I kept overlaying and idealizing until I had something that fit into me perfectly. Eventually I was supposed to meet someone who would tear through this image, breaking the seal like the prince through the briars and exposing the contents of my true heart. And until then I could not hear my heart through that seal but only misinterpret its muffled rumbling.

Why is it that love is supposed to be some great revelation, filling us with the sense that we were always wrong? "Everything I believed means nothing now. I was searching and now I've stumbled blindly across the answer." Why is this the way we are taught to think? It is as if those of us who are alone but think we are capable of love are necessarily and wholly wrong about our self-perceptions and ideas of what we want. We sleep in our shells or behind our walls, thinking we know what we want from the other side yet secretly waiting for the handsome prince to awaken us to a greater truth with his kiss.

We long to touch, but only our bodies know how. With falling in love comes a brief tang of this truth, and we begin to talk about discovery and nakedness and rapture. We begin to talk. But these initial downpours dry up, and we are compelled to settle down. Listen to the words, "settle down." I picture silt at the bottom of a lake. As a girl, I went swimming with a friend in a lake, and the bottom was not rock or sand or muck. It was more like the flesh of a pear, only warmer and darker. At the edge, the water casually ebbed against this silt floor and you could watch it, lifted, suspended, reflecting the light and then settling down into ripples. I stepped out into the water, my foot disruptive, clouding it to a marvelous glittering swirl.

Look at Me

Settle down. It seems the revelry ends there.

I have not gotten this far. The romantic in me is in-clined to believe that some people get it right; that for some, like my parents, settling down still has its twinkling moments. But the debater in me contends that this is usu-ally a malfunctioning, an incomplete gesture. Touching is difficult, occurring only at supreme and rare moments when we let go of everything and become weak. Let go of fear.

And so, my friend, my lover, I invite you to partake in an experiment, since I know you believe in experiments and that life should be only a series of provisional pro-cesses and products, fluctuating and unexpected. I invite you to bend your line to the curving whim of impossibil-ity, to fool planar dimensions and allow your parallel line to bend toward mine, to try to touch it. I don't know how. We will first, I think, necessarily wade through the thick stink of what-I-want and what-you-want, of expectation, pride, relative power, greed, anger, convention, trickery, loneliness, desolation, self-deceit, self-imprisonment. These are the components of fear.

And we will also have to work through a few basic terms. When I say I love you, I don't want you to misun-derstand. Love has its definitions in English, but I define it differently, and this act of re-characterizing an old word makes it confusing. Perhaps experts of language, and not I, should develop new words for this plethora of emotions, this sludge of passion and warmth and zeal that they grandiosely refer to as love.

I do not attempt to define love by what it is. I am only so smart. Rather, I humbly define love by what it is not. That amalgamation I described as fear is what motivates us, sadly, in most of our daily endeavors, but love is what is left when we let go of that fear, when we resolve to remain suspended in water or air, reflecting light. Love is matter and energy at once.

So here is my experiment. I want to see what happens if each of us, together, lets go of our fear. We will be honest and humble and unassuming, scientists mixing chemicals for the first time and observing whatever ensues, tame or tumultuous. Letting go of fear sounds like it should be pleasant, a child coasting down a waterslide feeling terror give way to thrill and rush. But fear anchors us to our world. Fear is a warm mug of cocoa and a bedtime story. But this comforting illusion of fixity is just this, an illusion. Letting go will not be pleasant. It will hurt. At first we will go to bed cold and thinking of ghosts. Imagine two parallel lines, merry and complacent, suddenly braving the unattainable, straining and seething toward each other, dripping the brutal sweat of failure but ceaselessly trying.

I invite you to stretch toward me, to fool this world that has tired of experimentation and settled down into contented ridges. I invite you to cheat, to have a nine-high hand and win. I invite you to complete in soul what we have begun in flesh, to be the butterfly and the storm at once. I invite you to yield to me as I will yield to you, piloting each other's infinities, waiting without fear to face the harsh swirling ferocity of it.

It makes a nice story, doesn't it? And what happens next? Do they find each other? Of course, of course. The lovers meet in the middle of a wide body of water, he steering his craft haphazardly, she on a steady course toward a moving target. At first, as she boards his boat, they cannot see each other, invisible as rays of infrared light, empty to each other as geodes. And a very real treasure lines the inside of him, but she is summoning a phantasm in the negative space she sees. For fourteen days they navigate the waters together and watch the sun travel a perpendicular path. For fourteen nights they sleep in the bowsprit, entwined in a common dream spun by the ghost in the stone.

In the dark left by the new moon they are shocked by what scintillates above them. What choking star is that, and how long have we been following it?

The address was not difficult to find. I searched through the drawer of my desk for a clean envelope.

THIRTEEN

"IAIN, I'M ALMOST READY. I just need to find my keys," I called out in response to the knocking. It was Sunday morning, and though we usually met at Pot and Kettle's he sometimes came to hound me when I was late.

"It's not Iain," came the white-chocolate voice through the closed door. Watching the moon fill out and begin to wane, I had fallen asleep the previous three nights in anger and frustration when the telephone kept not ringing and not ringing. Promising myself that I would attempt a normal Sunday, I was trying not to wonder about Jonas when he came. In a panic I pulled my hair back and hoped I did not look awful and let Jonas into my apartment for the second time. I tried to be stable. Stable as a boulder balanced on a precipice moments before a great quake.

Jonas looked pretty as ever, his linen suit impossibly crisp and his dark eyes purposeful. He shone like a square-cut topaz. I did not know whether to hug him, kiss him, shake his hand, clobber him. Is there an etiquette for one whose incisors are in your heart?

"Jonas, you're here. I didn't—I thought—I mean, I didn't know you'd come. I'm glad. We need to talk. I need to tell you something," I spurted before he had finished settling into my desk chair.

"You need to tell me something?" He was tiger-calm. "You think I don't know yet? You think my wife didn't call me immediately after she got your sick little letter?"

"Jonas, please!" I was using the snivelingly pathetic voice. "Jonas," I said placidly this time, "I was hoping I'd be able to tell you myself."

"Well, you didn't. You know why? Because my wife and I love each other. We're close. We trust each other, or at least she used to trust me. You fixed that, right?"

"That wasn't what I meant to do!"

"Oh, okay. You wrote a letter to my wife and told her that her husband slept with another woman, and you weren't *meaning* to ruin her trust in me? What did you *mean* to do?"

"I don't know. There was another letter that I wrote to you—"

"Well, perhaps you should have sent that one! I don't know, maybe even to me?"

"Are you going to let me finish? I wrote a letter to you because in all these months I haven't been able to loosen myself from you. You and I are connected. I know you experienced it that night at the observatory." I sounded miserable and trite. How was I supposed to explain myself?

"Connected? Dana, we spent one day together. This whole thing is just your pitiful way of trying to get back at me. That's what you are. Pitiful."

"You're the one who contacted me. You sent me wine! You thanked me for letting you communicate your passion! You wanted to see me for a little adultery while you were back here. If you're having marital difficulties you can't possibly blame me. It was your marriage to protect and your choice to bed me. All I did was tell the truth."

"It wasn't your business. If you had something to say, you should have said it to me."

"You're right. Maybe I should have sent that letter I wrote you. Maybe not. The envelope was all addressed and sealed and I was holding it over the open mailbox and I stopped myself from letting it fall. Then I went home, wrote the other letter, copied the address. I was scared."

"So you dealt with that by going behind my back and telling my wife?"

"Can I ask you something, Jonas? I mean, you don't have to answer, but we never even talked about your marriage when we should have. I was guilty too. I noticed your ring, but I felt like . . . like . . . I was I having such a wonderful time with you that I didn't want to risk it by mentioning your marriage, and I knew you were having a wonderful time too. I believed you must not have been happy in your marriage. Is that true? Because if you really are happy like you now say you are, and you were just playing or exploring with me, then I've done something wrong and I'm truly sorry. But—"

"Dana," he interrupted, shifting himself in the chair and fidgeting with the keys of the computer, "Obviously I'm not totally satisfied or else I wouldn't have done what I did with you. It wasn't even just the sex. I found you alluring from the first time I talked to you on the airplane. You're interesting and exciting, and I could tell you stories I cannot share with my wife because they'd hurt her. I could tell you about the real reason I bought the vineyard when she thinks it's some oh-shit-I'm-in-my-mid-thirties thing. I could go with you to the Eastern

Market, when she would have been pulling out her wallet at every other table. I was fascinated by you because I knew you had an appreciation for things I see."

"That's part of what I mean. There is something that joins us."

He breathed and crossed his arms to hold his shoulders before he responded, quietly.

"You still don't get it. We're not connected," he said, "But I'd be lying if I said all you did that day was bring something out of me that needed to be brought out, because that makes it seem too self-serving. I—when I was very little, my mother took me on a hike up a mountain and at the top there was a rock pool and a waterfall. My mom pointed at it and said, 'It's a waterfall, Jonas,' and I said, 'It's a wonderful!' 'Waterfall.' 'Wonderful.' And she said, 'Well, it is pretty wonderful, isn't it.' As restless as I was when I was that age, I stood with my mother for what must have been a long time, looking at the wonderful. That's you, Dana. You're a wonderful."

I looked at Jonas and felt wonder-full.

"You *are* a wonderful, Dana," he continued. "You see things. I felt that night like we were both really *looking* at the stars, like I really looked at the waterfall. It's a rare experience for me that I can be in the company of someone else and really feel like I'm at my most essential, but I did with you, from the first time we talked on the airplane."

"I knew it! I knew you felt that just as much as I did."

"But Dana, I can't be anything to you now."

"I always knew that too."

"Did you? I do love my wife. She's a very generous

144

and good-hearted person. She's willing to have a husband who spends many nights at an observatory, sometimes overnight, and uses the days to do equations. She handled all my moods when I was a grumpy doctoral candidate and still got me to take off the occasional afternoon so we could go see the giraffes at the zoo—I love giraffes."

"Yes." I was trying to derail him. "They manage to look ludicrous and graceful at the same time."

"Anyway, she might not be able to share some of my aspects, and I might not be able to show her the devil in my head, but she's endured me. I love her for it, and I *am* happy, and I don't like seeing her upset. You messed up this trustworthy thing that I have, or had. Why, Dana, if you understood that I was married and that no matter how close we got that night, it was only supposed to last that night?"

What was I supposed to tell him? I'm not afraid of you? It's okay? I've seen through to you and what I see has fire and a pitchfork, and I accept you? No. No. He decided a long time ago that he would rather compromise himself, shut that devil in his head within a tight iron prison, because this was a better fate than being alone. Late at night he hears the scratching sound of iron on iron, but he has learned to let it lull him to sleep. His fear, after all, is what lets him keep the woman who sleeps beside him every night. Breathe. Breathe. She is a cloud, maybe. He is a blast furnace.

And he knew he had not showed me the full surging scope of who he was, the mad spirits residing in every layer of his skin, but the fears were his, not mine. He had trusted me, if not himself. This trust was possibly the greatest compliment anyone ever had given me. And he had understood that I loved him. What more was there?

So what do I tell him? You were wrong, you can trust me? You should not have made that decision to marry someone who cannot see all that you are? I want to know you, and that is all? It doesn't work that way, not once you've made the choice against loneliness. And I understand that much; I know loneliness in all its parasitic and raging manifestations. How could I even ask him to go back on the decision that relegated loneliness to an iron prison next to the one that contained his soul? I would not do it.

"I love you, Jonas," I said instead, and I knew that in my voice he heard the scrape of his own iron on iron.

"You can't."

"I can. I do."

"What does that even mean?"

"It means I accept you. I care about you. I think about you, and I think about you in amazement. Who are you, and where are you, and what made you come to me? You're smart and you're fascinating and you too brought something out of me that I never share. With you I become—I don't know—*better*. Since meeting you, I've become better. I've been learning about stars, and wine, and I've been writing better and most importantly I've been reveling in the experience of my own life."

"Dana, I didn't do that. You did that. You might know a little bit about me but you don't know me. You haven't really seen what it's like to have my life. My wife has."

"I do see you."

"Maybe you saw something, and maybe what you saw is who I am, but if you really understood the things I need you wouldn't have sent that letter."

He was right.

"You're wrong, Jonas," I said, shuddering. "But I am sorry. I don't know what else to say or do."

"Don't do anything. I'll try to take care of this somehow, salvage my marriage, and you can try to salvage yourself. But you can't contact me again. You have to know that what we did was transient, and in order to continue our lives we can remember each other, but we can't do more than that," he said, rising and moving toward the door.

"One, two, three, four, five," I said softly.

"What?"

"Nothing."

"Aren't you supposed to count to ten when you're angry?"

"I'm not angry," I said, not wanting to explain the private panacea my father unwittingly had given me when I was two days old. "Just please don't leave me yet. I never wanted anything like a committed relationship, not from you. I just wanted to look at you a little more."

"Look at me? Okay, look at me."

I did, and I saw a man whose skin had the exact smell and color of Darjeeling tea, steeped for one minute in a glass mug and held up to bright sunlight. Everything about him was hard and square—his jawline, his shoulders—except that voice, and his dark eyes. Jonas like a square-cut topaz.

"I love you."

"I've got to go."

The adrenaline lasted for the time it took to escort him to the door of my apartment, turn the two locks and step inside. But as soon as I sat down on the couch, flustered, beaten and panting, I began to cry. Loud and wailing, until my whole body swelled.

What I remember from that day is standing in the kitchen after he left, eating hot fudge sauce straight from the jar and drinking Trapezium Estates wine straight from the bottle. I remember the sick feeling from finishing both, the wooziness of music coming though the steam in the bathroom when I took a shower to wash away the vomit. The convulsive tears. But for a moment, just when he left me never to return, I had a brief moment of seductive pleasure, a millisecond of chocolate-and-wine induced ecstasy, where I could have swooned and forgotten all about him. This is what I remember best.

And I remember wishing I had shown him my letters. Maybe if I had been able to indicate what I meant when I said I loved him, he would have appreciated me and wanted to stay. Could I have impressed him with those letters? In the beauty of my images, would he have seen the beauty of the writer? But I was feeling blunt and ragged and dirty as a used pencil eraser.

Where was Iain? Shouldn't he be worried about me by now? Shouldn't he have come here long ago with two cups of Pot and Kettle's coffee and tried to drag me out?

If I send the letter now he will get it by the time he gets back to San Francisco. And so, pressing back the thought that perhaps this letter would make him want me, I write out his address on an envelope for the third time, now with his name again and not hers.

Once upon a time I stood in the inverted bowl of an observatory, marveling at the rings and moons of Saturn, learning the ecliptic. It was a bright cool clear night in August, the night I split apart, breaking up like a celestial body so part of me could make that leap and stay with him. And I've seen him since, and my body has rejoiced that it converges once again, sleeping next to him in a white bed.

Yes, this is a story. It is make believe, and it is true. And one of my selves does know the heady scent of the peony by heart, and another the taste of blueberries; and one split my father's skull, and another my mother's womb; and one is breathless in the desert with my lover, and another is here alone, chronicling what might be my own history. I have no memories; I am no tightrope walker. I am a flock of white birds in flight.

I close the letter with a plea, for forgiveness and friendship. I ask him to visit me if ever again he comes to Washington.

What if he does come again? What if he had understood what it meant to experience the lure of an unlived life? I do not know what I would have chosen for him.

And if he comes to see me, will I want him to join me for another Sunday at the Market?

I am at my most appealing when I am sad. I have

seen, walking along streets, looking through bookstores, that men notice me more often after I've been crying, when the red in my eyes has faded just enough to make the irises look greener and the cool sorrow keeps them in a slight squint. Pain takes the intimidating pride out of my stature, and the lasciviousness in my glances is replaced by a Cinderella-at-midnight breed of desperation. "Come help me, I'm lost and I need you," I must cry out to these men, and they are drawn to me like water to water. I take advantage of their weakness perceiving my weakness. I use a soft voice and a down-turned, wistful smile to communicate my longings to them. "Yes, yes, you can fix everything," is the message. They respond. I've gotten sex in the middle of the day by this method. Of course, once the act is completed, I have profaned myself before them: the sad white beauty reduced to a ravished, rapturous woman. This is too much for them and they leave in distaste before I even get a chance to start writing.

I was exhausted. Mine was the anatomy of the depressed: pale, broken as a toy, windless and spidery as an underground cave, achy as an underground river. Nothing seemed interesting to me at all. I would get up, make coffee and think about all the boring things I would have to do before the day would be over, when I could lie in bed and wait to be bored to sleep. I was bored by my work, bored by men. I hadn't written in weeks.

Who could I fuck? Now that was interesting. I thought about the professor. I thought about the angles of his narrow body. I thought about his messy hair and messy office and wondered if there would ever be room on his floor to make love, or if we'd have to do it standing up, bent over the desk, papers crinkling as I tried to hold on during orgasm. I wondered if his frail old body would break as he thrust into me from behind.

Loneliness is staying too late at a bar, serenaded by the susurrations of the last drunken strangers and the exhausted lights that buzz with their own emptiness. Outside the shattered streetlights and cigarette butts are almost reassuring. You walk home, tying and retying the sash of your coat to protect you against the hush.

He was tired, and I told him to go to my bedroom to rest while I finished bringing the boxes of his clothes and books and photo equipment into my apartment. He had not told me before, but his townhouse had belonged to his father. After a weekend-long cocaine spree Iain got a visit from his ex-military dad, who seeing his son's condition kicked him out and put up the house for sale. I offered to have Iain stay with me for a few weeks while he replenished his body and his bank account.

He brought me a book from Sepia that said I was being too much of an enabler. I gave tacit approval of his weakness by hanging his thin sweaters in my closet and arranging darkroom space for him in the basement of my building. And instead of giving him a pillow and a blanket and relegating his slumbering self to the sofa, I invited him to my bed. The first night he was looking through his clothes for something suitable to sleep in— he used to sleep naked but he found this inappropriate now—and I retreated into the bathroom to shower. When I emerged, I found a pillow dividing the bed in half and Iain already asleep under a sheet.

Lauren   Porosoff   Mitchell

From the kitchen I heard the answering machine beeping. When I pressed the play button and heard Jonas's white-chocolate voice I shivered.

"Dana, hi. I'm calling to tell you I cannot see you again. I don't blame you anymore for what happened. I realize it was my fault, certainly more so than yours, and I'm sorry I wasn't more sympathetic to you. It's just that there's something dangerous about our chemistry, and even though I care about you very much, I don't think we can be friends. So I appreciate the invite, but honestly, even though I don't hate you, I have no interest in associating with you in any way. Sorry to be so severe. I hope you know I'll think of you fondly. Bye."

If you've never tasted the acridity of grief or known the strata of sorrow, can I get you to feel them when you have no memory as your referent? I warn you, but can I bring you to it? What does the death of a loved one smell like? What is the smell of the death of love itself?

Could science do it? Could we program the acoustic nerve to fire in exactly the right sequence to hear a wail of torment in an empty room? Will you pick up where I left off?

I could have said nothing in response to Jonas. I could have attempted to show him exactly where we were both wrong, but to reiterate my story of Jonas and I would have been futile. What was crucial was that I was never motivated by love for Jonas but by fear of not being loved. That fear was responsible for all the pain and anger that transpired. But that night, for the first time, I did something for Jonas purely out of love. Prune-fingered, I wrote him a letter, a fat drop of water from my shower-wet hair smudging some of the ink.

> *I appreciate your honesty, and I'll respect your wishes. I will always wonder whether, if we could have controlled ourselves that first night, we would have had the kind of friendship we probably both need. But as much as I wish I could take back the ways I have hurt you, I cannot, and I can only be grateful for the opportunity to see someone truly beautiful in you. Thank you for being that person, for allowing me to see that person, and for forgiving me, if not to the point of friendship, then at least to this point of lucidity. I will stop missing you, but I will always love you. Dana.*

I addressed and sealed the envelope, laying it neatly on my desk. Then I combed out my hair, tied it up and climbed into bed next to Iain, who was breathing so quietly I had to check his carotid artery to be sure he had not exhausted himself to death. I knew the light was coming in from the street and reflecting off of him, but it seemed to be his pale body itself that illuminated the room. I removed the pillow dividing the bed and lay close to Iain without touching him. Sensing my heat, he curled into me.

FOURTEEN

IAIN IS FLUSHED AND SMILING triumphantly as he explodes into the apartment like a starburst. From his backpack he begins unloading groceries: a whole chicken, four carrots, a bunch of celery, a big yellow onion. I can feel the amused little grin lapping at my mouth.

"I think I'm coming down with something," he says. "I thought maybe you'd be kind enough to make your mommy's magic soup."

"You forgot the parsley," I tell him, trying not to laugh.

"Hell, I'm lucky I remembered all this. I'll go back and get parsley," he says, about to pivot on his heel.

"Oh, and Iain? Could you get some zucchini and turnip and cabbage too? And a can of chopped tomatoes? And a lemon. Oh, and a bar of dark chocolate with nuts."

"Secret ingredient?" he sniffs.

"No, intense craving on the part of the chef."

When he returns breathing rudely, a beast with two bags, the apartment is already beginning to smell like my mother. Just to honor her, I am swaying from foot to foot, doing the occasional umbrella twirl. Iain frolics with me and helps me wash and chop the vegetables, and soon the smell of Mama is so thick I can feel her in the

155

steam. The soup needs to simmer for half an hour before I can add the parsley and salt and black pepper, and Iain takes advantage of the lull by putting on a John Fahey album, steering me into the living room, placing a square of chocolate in my mouth and slow dancing me to the slow, even guitar. His body feels as if it could crumble like cinnamon cake at my weight, but he moves me easily.

"Iain?" I say, my eyelids lazy. "Can you check the soup to make sure it isn't boiling over? Another accident would be bad."

He kisses both of my palms and goes into the kitchen. I drop down into my desk chair, lay my hands over the computer keys, close my eyes and think about Mama. It's almost time for the salt, I think, when I hear Iain's shriek from the kitchen.

"Oh my God!" he cries, sliding into the living room.

"What?"

"You will *not* believe what just happened!"

"What? Please don't tell me you had to put out a fire."

"No. I swear to God this happened. The salt—the container of salt on the counter? It just opened, and some salt came out and made a—like a spiral—through the air and landed in the pot. I swear to God."

"Iain, you're hallucinating," but already I am in the kitchen staring uncertainly into the soup.

"Taste it. Taste it and see if it tastes like there's salt in it."

"Okay." With the wooden spoon I swirl the soup, catch a piece of turnip in the broth, and taste. "There's definitely salt in there. Iain, are you fucking with me?

You put it in."

"No! Dana, I would not make this up. I wouldn't even know how much to put in."

"Mmmm. Small fistful." I feel hazy, as if I am waking from a nap on a hot beach, a bubbly aquatic haze erupting across my vision. Mama never told me how debilitating the Pulling can be. Maybe she was strong enough to control it, or maybe it made her mercury-mad, but if she was strong enough to make soup until her cancer metastasized, I can fight a Victorian-style swoon long enough to add the pepper and parsley, wait ten minutes, and serve Iain and myself with my mother's characteristic flourishes. Behind my eyes I am spinning, a spinning sparkling eight-spoked wheel, a fleshy octopus whirling in delight.

"I feel a little light-headed," Iain says, blowing on a spoonful.

"Must be all the dancing. Or maybe you really are getting sick. You'd better eat that while it's still hot."

But by the time I finished the soup and swirled the bowl so the remaining drops of broth coated the inside, I lost the euphoria in telling Iain what had happened with Jonas.

"I never really loved him," I told Iain, my voice stale from reciting the whole encounter. "How could I have? I only knew him for a day, and after that he was my creation. It's almost Jocastan, isn't it? I made him. I gave him life and breath. Somewhere in California there lives a man who has a wife and a wonderful job in universe discovery. I have no idea how he reacts to thunderstorms, or what kind of toothpaste he uses, or whether he played football in high school, or how he felt when he started to go bald, or what his favorite section of the paper is, or what his biggest fears are. I don't know what animates him, because the man I call Jonas is someone *I* animated. For myself. I fucked him for myself, so I could have the pleasure of sleeping next to someone I thought could love me."

"You were lonely," said Iain.

"Yes, and I still am. I still feel untouched. I have been with almost a hundred different men, but in so many ways I'm still a virgin. Except my color is not white but brown, like dirty water. They were just a bunch of dirty dishes who left their residue in my sink, and now the only thing inside me is dirty water."

"Well then, dirty water must be beautiful where you live."

I wanted to react to this, but I had to continue. "I took Jonas in because through him I could experience that touch."

"Dana, there's nothing wrong with wanting to be touched."

"Oh, no, but just listen to my words. 'I took Jonas in because.' In love there is no because. In love, or at least as I understand love, you just accept that person for no real reason. You just love them. This is supposed to be some obvious truth. I wanted something out of him. And I got something, but it was out of myself. Now I'm done creating. I'm empty."

It was not so much that she cared what he thought. She was not trying to impress him, not really. She had created an elaborate fiction, an otherworldly version of herself. That self had long, deliberate fingers, long enough to touch him wherever he went. That self had hair like a violent storm and skin like the surface of a lake. The perfection of that character bore down on her with great weight, and when she got a chance to live out her story she felt insecure, inadequate, because her fleshly self *was* inadequate.

The label on the file folder that sits on my desk reads "K0220" in my blue inked handwriting, from the Kerners' last name and the date they first came in. What I have to tell the Kerners is that K0220 will be a boy and a carrier, but not a victim, of Acid Maltase Deficiency. What else can I know? The Kerners will kiss and hug and maybe cry, and they'll thank me as they leave my office to go celebrate over some non-alcoholic beverages and plan for their baby boy who is due in three months. This is what I know. What I do not know, cannot possibly predict, and will not have a chance to see are the intimations on K0220's face, the efforts of his first words, the thoughts he has as he sits at his desk on his first day of school, the contours of his secret grief. What moment is this when I look at you? What possibilities will manifest? Do I see you?

Poring over the Kerner records, I think about a time, very early in my career, when a six-foot tall, pearly-haired and curvaceous girl knocked shyly on my office door even though it stood wide open.

"Karen." I recognized her immediately as an old friend from MIT who had lived in my dorm sophomore year. "Please, come in!"

"Hi, Dana." She crossed the threshold and took the

chair opposite me. She was quivering like a frightened puppy. From behind her back she produced a white peony. "This is for you," she said, setting the flower on my desk. "I remember how you always used to have peonies on your windowsill in college."

"Thank you." Instead of asking her what she was doing at my office, I waited for her to speak.

"I noticed in the class news last alumni newsletter that you're a genetics counselor."

"Yes."

"I came here to talk to you about my genes."

I got up and closed the door before asking, "What's going on?"

"You know what Huntington's Chorea is, right?"

"Yes," I said, sitting down and bracing myself. Chorea, from the Greek word for dance, came to be the common name for Huntington's Disease because those who suffer from it show involuntary bodily movements that can look like dancing. When I learned about it in a first-year genetics course at MIT, I thought instantly of my mother's dancing fits. Of course my mother's revelry was innocent, but still I developed a fascination for this rare genetic condition.

"My grandfather had it. My twin brother and I used to make fun of him and call him 'Dancing Grampy' until we learned about his condition. My father—his son—is fifty-one now and still hasn't developed any symptoms."

"Well, that's good. Most at-risks develop symptoms by the time they're forty-five, but there have been documented cases of symptoms emerging as late in life as seventy."

"I know. I also know that my father has a fifty percent

chance of getting it, and if he has it then I have a fifty percent chance of getting it, and if I have it, I have a fifty percent chance of passing it to my baby," she said, rubbing her belly fondly.

"You're pregnant now?"

"Five weeks. I just found out a few days ago."

"Does the father know yet?"

"Dana, I'm not even sure who the father *is*. I'm not exactly monogamous."

"I know how that is," I said, in a careless and un professional instant.

"I mean, I've slept with a lot of guys. A *lot*—I mean, college was nothing, and lately . . . I . . . I mean, I'm twenty-five years old. I'm a patent attorney now."

"Good for you."

"It's definitely not as exciting as it sounds. I don't think I even realized over the last few months why I've been so lax about birth control until I found out I'm go-ing to have a baby. I want this more than anything, but I want to know if I'm a Huntington's carrier so I can know whether the baby's at risk. Also so I can know whether I'll live long enough and be sane enough to see my grandchildren."

"That's a lot to have on your mind as a single mother with a blossoming career."

"I know. That's why I want to get tested. Can you do it for me?"

"Well, you should understand that there are special HD testing centers where they can give you the care you need. You should really get a complete neuro work-up and a psychological counseling session. I can't do that for you. Let me see if I can find the list of testing centers in Virginia and Maryland," I said, opening a desk drawer and scanning through papers.

"I already know about those," Karen sighed. "I don't want to do all that. I want you to do it for me. I trust you, and I know you can give me the support I need."

"Karen, of course I'll support you, but you should do this the right way. I always recommend to my clients that they bring a family member or a friend when they get screened. What about your dad? Your brother? What about trying to figure out who the baby's father is? I do paternity testing too."

"Dana, I don't even really want to know who the father is, and the fact that I'm pregnant means I'm going to have to ask my family for help anyway. Plus, I don't want to start up with Huntington's with my dad and my brother. They have their own ways of dealing with it."

"Well," I stalled, considering giving her a hypocritical speech on communicating with her family. Instead, I asked, "How have you been feeling lately? Have you noticed any depression or mood swings?"

"No."

"Any problems remembering things or unusual clumsiness?"

"I mean, I've always been a klutz. You cannot have forgotten that night at Beta Chi."

"But any unusual lack of coordination?"

"No."

These were questions a medical doctor should have been asking her to see if she had any early symptoms. "Have you noticed any twitches? Nervous tics or anything?"

"Nothing."

"Okay. Well, as you may know the test for HD is a blood test where we look at a segment of DNA on the short arm of chromosome four. If you have the gene for Huntington's we'll see a higher number of a specific repeated sequence. You should also know that if you don't have the gene, then there is no chance you can pass it on to your child, and that even if you do carry the gene, your child will have only a fifty-fifty chance of getting it."

"Right." She was still trembling.

"Karen, you know that your test results could affect your emotional well-being, and it's already a stressful time in your life because of your pregnancy. If you want, we can do an amniocentesis a little later in your term and find out if the baby you're carrying has the gene. If your baby does have the gene, then you probably do too unless the father is a carrier, which is highly unlikely. If the baby does not have it, then you have the security of that knowledge without having to live knowing that you will one day develop a disease for which presently there's no cure."

"Can you test me now and do the amnio if I have it?"

"Are you sure, Karen? I mean, you can go home and think about it and come back any time."

"I want to do it now. I've been wanting to do it for a few years now, but I didn't have the guts until I found out about this," she said, her hand on her belly again.

"All right," I sighed. "I know the technicians down in the lab. I'll ask them not to enter your results into the computer so you don't get billed. You should be saving your money for your baby, and you really don't want to report HD tests to your insurance."

"Oh my God, thank you Dana."

"We can't do it today. If you come back tomorrow I will have had time to make the arrangements."

"I think I can wait until then. Thank you so much, Dana," she said, standing up and turning to go. "You're a saint."

A saint. Karen did not keep in touch, and I never got to see the baby born. I do not even know if the child is a boy or a girl, since thankfully Karen's blood work came back spotless and I never saw the fetal chromosome profile. What a job I get to do. I could have been a chemical mixer like my dad or a star scanner like Jonas, but instead I chose the bedlam of human genetics. I marvel, as I examine these printouts and test results and electron microscope photographs, that these little blotches produce the codes for people. In the cryptograms of their four-letter alphabets they answer some of the questions. "Will my baby be okay?" they often ask. "Is it a boy or a girl?" they sometimes want to know, and sometimes they say, "We want the sex to be a surprise." When I tell the parents that their child will grow up free of any discernable genetic diseases, they usually say something to me like "Bless you." But I am no saint. I created nothing; I suffered nothing; I only translated their own extraordinary language.

Heisenberg's Uncertainty Principle says the surer we are of a point's velocity, the less sure we can be of its position. This principle of physics ensures that even knowing everything about a system—a person's genetics and environmental circumstances, for example—we still could not predict its path(s) with certainty. But perhaps God is that which *can* be certain. Physics, after all, is a scheme of communication, capable of *describire* but not *facere*. What knowledge lies beyond the linguistic capacities of physics remains the province of God.

My father is a man of disciplined discovery. He taught me to believe in the story that was already there, the scripted certainty of the universe. And now he is proud of me for my bilingual endowment, my business of reading people their own stories. When he calls me he always wants to discuss some new article on genetic research, on the remedial possibilities of reverse transcription or gene therapy. "It won't be long before you can cure some of those awful diseases you find in your clients," he likes to remind me. I read these stories with titles like K0220, constructed and knowable as any narrative, but soon I will see them rewritten.

She had created an elaborate fiction.

I stand up and look out the window for a long time, running my hand over the butterflies so they scatter twinkles of fugitive light across the office.

My father the chemist, my father the inventor, rifling through boxes in the basement for my mother's blue dress. I had seen pictures of her, stunning beside my father, curvy and full-lipped and buoyant, and I wanted to wear the dress to a dance at college. I had driven home from Boston just to get the dress, having given my father weeks of forewarning, but now here he is, afraid of the boxes, rummaging only when forced by circumstance and with me to protect him from the wreckage of memory.

"Dad, look!" I cried, producing my tiny navy blue wool coat, smelling like a wet sheep but with traces of my mother's perfume. He grunted a quick acknowledgement of my voice, if not of the coat, afraid to pry open the sealed catacombs of my childhood because this would invoke her even more. I looked through the remaining contents of the box, the little blouses and corduroy pants, stifling my unfamiliar homesickness.

"Help me move this bed," my father addressed me finally. I used the well-developed muscles in my arms and legs to pry the rust-spotted frame from my old bed away from more piles of boxes.

"Daddy," I said, when finished and dusty I began to open a box.

"What?"

A cricket had wandered into the house, seeking the heat of the boiler.

"There's an enormous insect about to crawl onto your foot. Don't move."

But he stamped, and the large cricket fled in an effortless hopscotch to some hiding place in the cardboard underbrush.

"Dad! I like crickets. He just wanted to come look at the dress, if we ever find it."

He put down the old chipped teacup he had produced and crossed the obstacle course we had made of the basement and began stroking my back. "Dana," he said, "I miss your mother."

"I know, Daddy. I do too."

"She would have floated that cricket away from me and it would have trilled for her in gratitude."

"I know, Daddy." It was the only time he ever admitted to the Pulling.

"She would have known exactly where to find the dress."

"She probably would have helped me try it on and danced me all over the house. I would have had a better time dancing around the basement with her than I will at this stupid dance. Everyone is going to get drunk and sloppy. Maybe I should just wear the green dress I have at school."

"Dana, if you can drive all the way up here and wrest my old bones out of the lab and down to the basement, I'm going to find your mother's dress for you. You'll look beautiful in it." He smiled, patted my back and continued his search.

FIFTEEN

THE WAY SHE DRIVES, she has her left foot up next to the steering wheel, and she rests her left elbow on the bent-up knee and steers with her left hand. Her right hand is cupped around his, their fingers interlaced. When they hold hands like this she notices that juxtaposed with his broad soft fingers her fingers appear longer, slimmer, more elegant than usual. She could be a pianist, she thinks, or a noblewoman with long white fingers like that.

He is giving his opinion of a poem, but she cannot listen to his words. This is strange, she admits to herself, because she was waiting so long to recite her favorite poem to him and imagined many times the way her soft voice would breathe out each of the words and how she would listen excitedly as he gave his interpretation. But now, as the car met the curves of the dark highway, she could not listen for the meaning of his language and heard only the mellifluous syllables.

"Something's wrong," he interrupts himself.

"No, I was just listening," she says, telling two lies.

She pulls her right hand away, steers with it, and cradles her head in her left.

"You can tell me or not, but something is wrong."

"No," she says, this time truthfully.

"I believe you," he assures her.

"I love you," she wants to tell him, but doesn't.

"Can I show you my new ones?" With a grin as proud as his tone, Iain produced from a big folder a series of photographs and began handing them to me one at a time as they swathed me like a net. Pigeons blanketing the roof of a beat-up mint green van. A woman lounging back on the Dupont Circle fountain, shielding her eyes from the sun by holding up her tiny child. An immaculate businesswoman trying to eat a sloppy sandwich on a park bench beside a man with a shopping cart full of coats. A cream-colored cat in a brick-framed window. Three men packing up the peanuts and pears remaining on their vending table. Nuns' habits whipping in the wake of a truck turning down K Street. A sad collie sprawled among feet and bicycle wheels.

"You're good," I told him.

"I have potential."

He came and without warning began to work his origami of my torn-paper body. I became a tulip, perhaps, or a rose, intricately folded.

And if he were to leave me I would crumple.

That night, eyes wide in the dark, I saw a crumpling flower and rolled over in frustration. But coiled in a thick sleep, I dreamed of running in a huge howling pack. I knew they were female because of their breasts, but they were muscular and green with grotesque faces. They were insect-women, running together toward some place where they could finally rest their bodies that pounded in dark flurrying unison against the city pavement. It was the pounding that woke me, or rather its muted echo like a heartbeat filtered through muscle and skin.

Somewhere in every story there lies a buried diamond.

Iain troubled me like a sick feeling in the middle of the night. I would sit up straight in the bed and watch the way the passing cars outside skimmed bands of light over his sleeping body.

Morning. He is sleeping in my bed and I am cooking French toast for him, my hands sticky with egg batter. He wanders into the kitchen, saying the smells of cinnamon and vanilla woke him. Drowsily he sits at the marble-topped ice cream table and cuts up the puffed slices and eats them slowly, pausing after lifting each bite to watch the syrup drizzle in fat amber drops onto the plate. I am doing dishes by hand even though I have a dishwasher, and the hot steam coming up from the plates fogs my silver wire-rimmed glasses and curls my red hair and slicks my face with a fine sweat and lifts my morning scents from the thin skin of my neck.

"You're beautiful," he says foggily.

"I love you," I say.

He looks at me wonderingly, like Jonas must look when he finds a new star he should have seen many months before.

"Really?"

"Yes."

"I love you too," he says, and in one fluid motion he is up from the table and in the kitchen beside me, covering my lips and shoulders with kisses, rubbing his neck on my neck and kissing my mouth so heavily that I can taste his soap. I pink from the scratchiness of his stubble on my skin.

He takes the red glass tumbler from my left hand and the sponge from my right. He is about to put the glass on the drying rack but then, reconsidering, he holds it up to the bright light coming through the window.

"If we have a daughter we'll name her Ruby," he says. The light expands in red ripples on his face. "She'll be a red-headed firestorm, like her mother. She'll burn."

"And if we have a son?"

"I hope he won't be skinny like his dad."

I laugh. "But what will we name him?"

"What name do you like?"

"You know, my favorite name for a man—besides Iain, of course—is Joaquin, but for the son of an Ashkenazi Jew and a blue-eyed Scot? Although you are part Spanish."

"Not enough to name my son Joaquin," he says with an exaggerated accent. And then, putting down the glass and surrounding me with the trellis of his arms, "How about Alexander?"

I grimace.

"Samuel? Wallace? What's Anaz—what did you call yourself?"

"Ashkenazi Jew? There are three kinds of Jews, Ashkenazi, Sephardic, and Mizrakhim. If you have other Jewish friends, they're probably Ashkenazis—those are the ones from Russia and Eastern Europe. *Mizrakh* means east, and the Mizrakhim are Jews from Asia. Sephardic Jews are from Spain or Portugal originally. Now they live mostly in Israel."

"So we could be distantly related?"

"Not really. Not unless Grandma Saint was part Jewish."

"Actually," Iain says, hesitating, "She was. It was the

big family scandal. When we were calling each other making the arrangements to go to Rome, the big topic of conversation was whether the Church would find out that their new saint was married to a Jewish woman."

"No kidding. But the Sephardic Jews were kicked out of Spain in 1492."

"I remember hearing something about that. *Abuelita* didn't talk much about her Jewish mother, but she did say that her mother's family felt connected to Spain for generations even when they lived in Peru. They moved back to Spain and raised *Abuelita* and her brothers and sisters Catholic, and when *Abuelita* came to New York she met my grandfather, who is from Scotland also. He was a devoted Protestant."

"So, your *Abuelita* is your father's mother?"

"Mother's mother. Dad's a full-blooded Scot, remember?" Iain says, puffing up his voice.

"*Abuelita*'s mother was Jewish?"

"Yes."

"Well then, according to Jewish law," I say, starting to giggle, "You're technically Jewish too. It descends through mothers. Wait till you tell Grandma Saint that she's really Jewish!"

He starts laughing too. "*Barukh ata? Oy vey! Shalom!*"

And we are both laughing until we can't breathe.

"Well then, how about something Hebrew if we have a boy?" I ask when finally I can speak. "I love the fact that 'Emmett' means truth, but it's such a stodgy name."

"I like Emmett."

"Isaac? Benjamin? Malachi? Seth?"

"Malachi."

"It means, 'my angel.' "

"Perfect."

"Well, I hope we have a girl anyway. I love the name Ruby. Ruby Lark McArdle."

The story should end in the two making love all morning in the bright apartment and lounging naked as cats in the patches of hot light. But instead she finishes the dishes, showers, kisses his face and goes out all day, afraid to come home. The sky is too white, a great sheet of blank paper waiting for a careless child to spill ink all over it. Treetops provide a chaotic breakup of the pallid spread, but even through the mesh of branches the sky expands alone and empty, befriended only by the occasional puff of sour city smoke. But life walks like the dead, color has drained like the blush from a condemned man's cheek, and the sprightly urban dwellers silently have fled, seeking the spectrum of elsewhere.

Pretending for my own benefit that I had errands throughout the city, I went shopping all day and bought nothing. By night it had turned cold outside and I acknowledged that it was winter. Lights from the bank on Dupont Circle broke through the massive blue night in a harsh orange: 6:24 . . . 7°C . . . 45°F . . . 6:25 . . . 7°C. . . . I stood hypnotized by those flashes of numbers that cut time and temperature into convenient units. Celsius was the metric unit for temperature, always making the world seem colder and simpler. Thirty-seven degrees Celsius was normal body temperature, but I felt my body cooling, freezing under the bank's trivializing lights, beginning to numb as if someone had shot up my whole life with a strong anesthetic. I had flicked off my emotions, watched as they turned to the greenish afterimage that stays behind eyes after the television is switched off, and concentrated on the shadows that were left.

I decided to go to one of the Georgetown bars, maybe pick up a college kid who was seeking to lose his virginity. In high school I had acquired a nickname, "the devirginator," and perhaps it was time to reclaim my title. Perhaps the dark and slick-haired boy who had replaced Randall in the drosophila lab would be there. Perhaps he would want to have a little encounter in the bathroom. I pictured him going out through the narrow splintered door, his corduroys wrinkled and a moist paper towel stuck to one of his expensive shoes. That image was enough to cheer me.

On an overheated bus, sitting amid faceless black wool overcoats and staring blankly at the back of the seat in front of me, I listened as the bus's empty hum intermixed with people's whimpering. Two middle-aged women boarded the bus and sat in the seats across from mine, glowing in their primary-colored coats like new crayons. Fervently they were discussing the best places in town to get facial peels. Where was I? And more importantly, did I want to be there?

I was a mole that had spent too much time fruitlessly burrowing through the ground, whose star-shaped nose was just breaking the surface. I got off the bus, crossed the street, and caught another bus toward home.

I would never claim to understand the lines (or spirals or circles or tesseracts) of causality reaching from one event to another. What I do know is that some things are closely and mysteriously connected, and that those connections penetrate and infiltrate and live above our heads and beneath our skins.

As an embryo (God knows how many cells I was made of then), I traveled to Spain, hearing the quick beat of a pulsing language beyond my mother's heart. The faint music, the rumbling digestion of paella, but I could not taste the saffron. And then—what?—did I kick her? Was it because I sensed Iain's ancestry? Did the world sense my desperation and send its message to the lost Jewish daughter, telling her to marry the lonely Scottish soldier? Did my tiny kicks alert my own Mama too? Was it she who Pulled Iain to me? Did she know?

Feeling pure after a shower, I put on a thin blue V-neck and white shorts, pin up my soaked hair and lie flat on the bed, my cheek against the sheet. Iain too has wet hair, having showered just before me. He is sitting on the floor, leaning against the bed and reading. I feel the magnetic energy building in my left shoulder, and soon he reaches back with his right hand, still able to read by pinning the book to the floor with his foot, and he strokes my shoulder and collarbone.

Then he says, "You smell so clean."

I say, "You too."

He lifts up his foot, allowing the book to flutter shut, and lies down on top of me, his front to my back. I wonder what it would be like to make love to him, what it would be like to experience the jut of his hip bones dimpling my soft thighs. He is so narrow. Would I feel him at all? Would I be able to wrap my legs tightly enough around him that we would be able to touch with our entireties? Or if I spread my legs wide enough, he would be able to move in and out of me so slowly with nothing else touching. His body would be smooth and I would look up at the sheer surface of him. I would not feel the physicality of his outermost layer of skin touching mine, not feel the pulse of his hot muscles, but I would feel something in the charged air around us, some transference. Our skins, devoid of the sweat and strain of each other's desire would act as perfect receptors for each other's energy.

Underneath Iain, I feel a short interruption in the steady oscillations of breath that have been breaking over my neck. His quick gasp, and I know he is having trouble breathing the air I infused with our ecstasy. That, or he is trying to take it in all at once. My own audible suspirations relax him until I feel the press of him but not the weight. We lie still like that until our breathing synchronizes.

SIXTEEN

HIS DOOR IS SLIGHTLY OPEN, but still I push it so I can see a sliver of him as I say, "Professor Fowler?"

"Yes?" And when I reveal myself he says, "Dana. Please, come in. Have a seat. I've been wondering when you'd come again."

"I came."

"I see that. How did you like the book?" He is blazing today and the butterflies quiver above him.

"I liked it. Thank you. And thank you for the butterflies. I should have said this earlier." I could have made an excuse for my delay, but I did not.

"I was about to have some wine. Join me?"

"Sure." There is not enough hesitance in my voice as I lean forward to watch him.

The jug he pulls from under his huge cluttered desk is printed with Greek letters. He fills two tin cups, hands me one and settles with his in the withered chair, his gaze secure on me all the while. I thank him for my wine and let it barely touch my timid lips.

"A little drink in the afternoon?" I tease. "Isn't this too stereotypical for an academic?"

"Yes. How do you like this foray into the ranks?"

"I'm enjoying it. In fact, can I have a piece of paper?"

He pushed his blue pad and a chewed-up, blunt pencil across the desk and I write: "I am having a splendid afternoon drinking with Professor Fowler." I hand him the note.

"I like your handwriting," he says. "Not too girly, but feminine. Graceful even. I like the word 'afternoon' especially. I like the way you make your *F* and double *O*," he says, but he is looking at me. "Can I keep it?"

"The note?"

"Just the 'afternoon.' May I?"

"Of course."

He tears the word carefully from the rest of the page and hands the remaining paper, which now says "I am having a splendid . . . drinking with Professor Fowler" back to me, places my 'afternoon' into his wallet and resumes his drinking.

I left something of myself with him. He kept the word, 'afternoon,' in my handwriting, tucked between the leather folds of his wallet. In pencil it was not fixed the way ink would be, but afternoon is a transient thought. I believed it unfair, that he should have something so uniquely mine in his possession, that at any moment he could leaf through the receipts and reminder notes and business cards and find a tiny slip of ragged-edged paper on which the word 'afternoon' was scrawled in my own lettering. He possessed a part of me as surely as if he owned a part of my body itself—a living fragment, a traceable relic.

I leave something of myself with them. The rule that matter can be neither created nor destroyed has always fascinated me, that the universe has a limited supply of building materials with which it invents and reinvents itself every day. Perhaps there are molecules that once belonged to your body that now belong to mine. It is almost a filthy thought, that constantly we are disintegrating and reintegrating using each other to rebuild. But it comforts and excites me—"body to body" and "star to star" sound better, feel better than "dust to dust."

They were in me.

Fowler and I sit leaning over the desk and sucking at the wine for a long moment after he has put away my word. Then he says, "So, now that you know you're surrendering your afternoon, how do you plan to spend the rest of it?"

"Well, I don't know. How were you planning on spending yours?"

"I thought I'd take you flying."

"You're a pilot?"

"I walked to work today so we'll take your car to the airport. It's not far. If we're going up we shouldn't finish this wine. 'No bottle to the throttle,' " he says, leaving the almost full cup on the desk and starting for the door. And then, turning his slender body to where I am still sitting, "You coming?"

It was not on a signpost, and had I not been scanning the road for the turtles that sometimes crept out I never would have seen the hand-painted wooden sign with its inviting dark blue lettering. "Plane rides today." Without thinking, I spun the steering wheel, skidding on the barely paved road and turning up the narrow driveway.

I could just make out the songs of late birds through the windy rush in the four open windows. My skin was hot even in the cold and I was beginning to feel dizzy. The professor was staring straight ahead.

The driveway kept sloping and twisting just when it appeared to be nearing a terminus. Scarring what once must have been swamplands, the road was rutted and muddy almost to the point of thwarting us, but my Vermont back-way training served me well. In first gear we progressed past another sign like the first one toward the field that was not a field.

"You know," he said, "All runways point north-south."

"Really? I like that," and I imagined the tiny line segments like pick-up sticks, flat and parallel to the imaginary meridians that sectioned the earth like a grapefruit.

A few cars and a beaten white van were parked haphazardly near a small red house, and dandelions mottled the 1800-foot grass strip with yellow and white. Tiny airplanes swayed in their row by the runway, hard white ropes preventing the wind from kidnapping them. One man stood by an airplane tightening its ropes, his beard rebellious. A second bulky, white-haired man squinted at the bright sky and I had to stare hard in the direction he watched to see the glint of an airplane's wing. It was this second man we approached.

"Gordie! Good to see you," he said when he noticed us standing beside him. "Going up? There's a strong crosswind today, but nothing you can't manage."

"We're just going for a little while, maybe do a few touch-and-gos."

Look at Me

I never got an introduction, but I cast a quick smile at the man as we turned to go to the professor's little two-seater airplane.

It was a cool, blustery day, and during the preflight check I imagined I would be freeze-dried by the wind slapping the runway. We walked around the airplane, a little Cessna 152, tied to the ground but bobbing and writhing over it like a helium balloon tied to a small child's wrist, or like the child herself squirmy in her seat at school, wanting to fly away.

"This airplane has a lot of lift," the professor explained. "She wants to fly." He proceeded to clarify every detail of what he was doing, running his windchapped hand over the leading edges of the wings, checking inside the engine for birds' nests, measuring the oil and draining a little gas to look for water bubbles. I watched, simulating fascination with this painstaking process of inspection, but really I was restless as the airplane to get in the air. That, and I was watching the turquoise gleam of the professor's eyes, watery from the cold wind.

But it was clear enough for our initial takeoff to be smooth, and hovering over Maryland I could not even think anymore. Over the old headset, the only means of communication between Professor Fowler and I, all I could say was "Wow," over and over, like a birdsong. The professor showed me how the yoke and pedals controlled the rudder and ailerons, and together we guided the plane down the Potomac River, using its twisting course as a road to follow. In the winds it was difficult to keep it steady, but I managed, and then I noticed the old professor's hand was not even touching the yoke.

"You mean I've been flying it alone?"

"For about fifteen minutes now."

I looked at him in disbelief, his spindly insect body with its wide wings.

"I told you, the plane wants to fly. You're just helping." When I smiled at him he said, "Watch the sky. You should always be looking for other planes."

How does it feel to fly? The night before I went flying in a light plane with the professor, I dreamed I could fly all on my own. My bones became hollow like a bird's and my body soared. Dreams of flight are supposed to signify sexual fantasies, that same kind of orgasmic letting go, that floating above the surface of the world, that bodily transcendence, that superhuman impossibility. Surely that was part of it, even if I had to awaken the next morning alone, blinking away the last images of him and reminding myself that his presence had been weightless.

How does it feel? In a 747 you cannot even tell; you feel the initial rush at takeoff as the ground expands and the life on it shrinks and fades. You reach cruising altitude, you sip from a tiny plastic cup of soda and watch the in-flight movie, maybe you read for a while, and maybe, if you're lucky, you meet someone to help you pass the time inside the airplane's body. The plane itself is so heavy, so controlled, that you can hardly tell you're in the air. At 36,000 feet you might as well be sitting on a bus. In a light plane you can tell, and for that inscrutable moment you feel both the roughness and the peace of knowing all your lives at once, skipping and stumbling over them like an airplane coasting over pockets of air, the infinity of you spreading and swirling like an atmosphere. You are no longer made of flesh and metal but of something lighter, becoming something that does not exist but is always on the verge of existing. You touch the yoke and delicately press the pedals, and your direction changes. Three hundred and sixty solid degrees of possibility for movement and a sky's insistence. The plane wants to fly, and your heavy body is overwhelmed with your opportunity to elevate. You surrender to the forces of physics. Touch and go.

In the car I ask the professor if he has time for a cup of coffee. He says he does, that an old man like him would only go home and take a nap after such a strenuous activity as flying. I convince him that he will be more comfortable if we get something from Pot and Kettle's and take it back to my apartment. We are sitting on the floor, drinking our coffee through the tiny slits in the plastic lids of our cups and eating dark chocolate cake. The way he sits, leaning against the couch with his knees up, I cannot believe he is as old as he claims to be.

I put four cold fingers on the back of his neck and he says, "You have bad circulation."

"I know," I whisper.

We sit like that, drinking our coffee and watching the sun settle over the monuments, until we hear the key turning in the first lock, then the second. Guiltily I remove my hand from Fowler's neck and twist around, peering over the rim of the couch to where Iain will make his entrance.

"Oh. Hello, I'm Iain. I live here too," he says, moving toward us with a hand extended, as for a handshake.

He uses it to help the professor to his feet.

"Gordon Fowler," the professor says, shaking Iain's hand. "I teach at the university where Dana does her fine work."

I wonder if Iain and Professor Fowler in their twinned skinniness are having the same drugged, dreamy feeling I am having, my body's movements jerky and involuntary as a marionette's, my mouth cramped and contorted, my brain static.

"Dana?"

"What?"

"I said, thanks for the coffee. I had a great day," says someone whose form focuses into Gordon Fowler's.

"I had a wonderful day too," I say. "And I should be the one thanking you. That was amazing."

"Well, I'll have to take you again. Stop by my office any time. And Iain," he says, turning, "Have a good night."

What if Iain had not come home at that moment? Would I have continued to allow my cool fingers the pleasure of the professor's skin? Would I have kissed him, arched naked up to him so he could feel me, invited him to the breath and breadth of me? And how would I have felt later, the clothes re-donned and the trash taken out and the stains sprayed with soap and the old man gone and my body washed clean of the smell of sex, when Iain did return? What involuntary vocal guilt would have betrayed my secret? What undestroyed evidence—hidden deeper in my flesh than the professor was able to probe, fused and intermeshed like viral DNA to the code of my soul—would have given me away?

After we hear the professor's footsteps recede down

the stairwell, Iain gives me a scathing look and flings himself on the couch without taking off his jacket. I look at him and want to kiss him for a long time. Instead I sit down next to him, put a hand on his back and say, "You're home early."

"Sorry I spoiled your date. I didn't know you were into the Father Time look."

"Iain, he's just a friend! We work together. We were just hanging out."

"Well, I come in, and the two of you are sitting on the floor in the dark. You were having *dessert*, Dana! What am I supposed to think?"

"What exactly is it about hanging out with a friend and eating chocolate cake that immediately translates into fucking him?"

"I don't know, Dana. You're the one who said you were fucking him." Shrugging my hand away he gets up and slumps toward the kitchen.

"I love you, Iain," I say as I follow him, telling the truth but feeling like I am lying somehow. "You're the only man I want. My relationship with the professor is platonic. I promise."

"Oh, I forgot. Because you'd never fuck another man. Nobody gets past your chastity belt."

"Iain, that's not—"

"Not fair? No, what's not fair is that I've been living with you for the past month and sleeping in your bed and telling you I love you and I know you're still going out and fucking other men, and all I ask is that you not do it in the same bed where we sleep or on the same floor where I danced with you or in this same fucking kitchen where we thought up the names for our children!"

187

"It's my kitchen." My tone is aloof, disdainful, but I am scared.

"Okay. It's your kitchen. Why don't you go out and find someone to fuck in it? It's still early."

"You're jealous, aren't you? You want to fuck me, Iain? You want me to suck your cock?" I move toward him and he waves me away.

"No, actually, I don't." When I only smirk he adds, "I don't ever want what we do to be the same as what you do with those men."

He sits back on the couch, his head in his hands. I want so badly to sit next to him, to run my hand over the soft fuzz on the back of his head, but I stay very still. So still that I can feel my muscles wanting to shiver. When finally I speak, the shivering emerges in my voice.

"I don't understand, Iain. Why are you still here?"

"What do you mean, why am I still here? Because I love you."

"You love me? You don't love me. How could you love me? What the hell do you even see in me? I know it's not this luxury apartment."

"What do *I* see in *you*? Let me show you something." From under the couch he produces a bag full of white powder. "Guess how much coke this is."

I can only stare at the bag.

"Guess!"

"I don't know."

"Guess how much money it cost."

I don't want to sound completely stupid so I overestimate, "Five hundred."

"Two thousand."

"Two thousand!"

"Sold! To the cute red-head," and he tosses the bag at me. I dodge out of the way as if it were an attacking cobra. Iain laughs as I stand eyeing the bag as if it will leap up at me.

"Pick that up off my floor. You promised me you'd never bring that trash into my home!"

"I know," he says, and the shame under his skin is audible.

"Pick it up!"

He drops to the floor and crawls to where the bag is, but he can only sit looking at it. I sit down with him and hug him tightly.

"I'm sorry, Dana."

"Iain, how long has that been there? Are you okay?" I do not have to force concern into my voice.

"It's been there since I moved in, but I haven't touched it."

"Why didn't you just get rid of it?"

"Why didn't you just stop fucking other men?"

"I didn't fuck the professor!"

"You know, I don't even care. I mean, I care, obviously, but when I walked in here and saw you with him I knew you would have fucked him if I hadn't come home, but I felt absolutely nothing. I know you've been with other guys since we've been—I don't know—together?—but I never did anything about it. Not coke, not drinking, not even finding some girl I could use for revenge. Nothing. I never thought to."

"Maybe you just had your own way of dealing with it. There's no prescribed way of dealing with pain."

"But Dana, I felt no pain. Some nights lying next to

you, or before we lived together when I was alone, I would actually force myself to think about you, what you look like, where you went at night. I even tried to picture you taking some other guy's dick, but it did nothing to me. And that night at my old house when we tried to have sex and then you left, I knew you were out finding some other guy. I kept saying to myself, 'You love her. She won't sleep with you but she'll sleep with everyone else in the city,' and trying to make myself cry. Do you have any idea what it feels like when you're supposed to be feeling something but all you can think of is that you're hungry and you wish the gyro place down the street delivered? Or—I don't know—the fact that your wool socks feel scratchy?"

The muscles of my chest spasm with joy for knowing that someone *sees*. My fleshly self, rising. "Yes. Actually, I know exactly what that feels like."

"How do you deal with it?"

"I don't. How do you?"

"I don't either." He pauses, picks up the bundle of cocaine and says, "Can you believe this shit? Will you flush it for me?"

"Are you really going to quit?"

"I'm really going to try."

"Well, you're not going to replenish your stash, right?"

"I don't have the money to buy more unless I steal from you," he chirps.

"Well, don't do that!"

"I don't even know why I bought this, but I don't want to look at the stuff ever again. I don't need to. So, have you figured it out yet? What do you see in me?"

"I see you. I love you."

"I see you and love you too, Dana."

"That's why you're still here."

"Exactly. So what happens next?"

"I don't know. I don't trust myself not to hurt you. What if I hurt you?"

"Don't hurt me."

"Iain, it's not going to be easy for me."

"Oh, because you're the one who has to quit the most addictive substance in the world."

"I thought that was nicotine. You know, I can't promise anything about what I'll do. The most I can promise is that I'll try to learn how to love you the right way, and that I'll try to stay whenever I feel the urge to bail. Is that what love means?"

"Maybe."

"Tell me what I can do," I whisper.

"You can flush the coke down the toilet."

"Okay, Iain, but I want you to do it with me. And I want you to try to trust me and help me trust myself."

"I do trust you. You've only ever shown me you. And, the only letter you ever wrote me you actually sent to me."

"Don't even joke!" I smile. "Anyway, you never responded to that letter. I had to track you to your place of employ. What if I hadn't? We never would have met again."

"So not true. I looked you up and went out to see you the night right before. But I ran into some of my friends on Seventeenth Street and they convinced me to have a beer with them, which turned into two and three and I got too drunk. Not that that stopped me from wandering over to your place. I was a mess, but I remember

I was dropping my empty bottle and screaming and yelling and falling down laughing 'Please help me, Dana.' But as you know, I didn't find you that night because I split before someone called the cops and had me arrested for public intoxication."

I can only look at him.

"I never told you that story?"

"No," is all I say.

"Well, I did try to find you, but then you came and found me."

We steady each other to stand up and get to the bathroom, and there we sit on the floor and the toilet is crooning and the water is sucking the cocaine down in a white whirl. Iain looks up and I look at him, and I hold up one little finger toward him. He offers his and we touch with the smallest parts of our bodies, fingertip to fingertip.

"Look at me," he says. He is still making love to me, slowly, his hips slow as a continent. What underboiling intensity is creating that continental drift? What violence will be done when he earthquakes and volcanoes? Is that ash and lava that I feel, the salt and sweat of him? Is that a mountain I feel him pushing up from inside my chest? My God, is that a whirlpool he opened up in my belly, the pleasure funneled down to a single point until—until—(he closes his eyes)—is this how the world felt when God created it?

"Look at me," I hear again, softer and farther away this time, echoing through the silverblue cloud of him. "Look at me," and a cool hand touches the magma of my flushed face, solidifying it. I have taken a new form.

Look at Me

"Look at me," he continues to say, and under his cool touch I am able finally to obey. Here I am above him, my red hair as sailors' ropes pulled knotted and kelp-covered from the depths of the sea, my body damp and scaly and glistening as a mermaid, clear as water. And in an instant he evaporates, becomes his cloud-self again only to recondense on me in waves of light, cycles of color.

I was sitting naked at the foot of the bed, looking at my toes, riffling them like the fringe of an old throw pillow, when he woke and saw me crouched oddly over my feet.

"Look at this," I said, snapping the digits of my second toe back and forth. "It break dances." His eyes are opening and closing like broken garage doors. "Look!"

"Okay. Must look." He clambered down from the bed and moved his head in closer.

"It's so ugly."

"I kind of like it. It looks like a baby alien finger."

"Yes! You know," I said, positioning my pinkie next to that second toe, "Sometimes I do this and I think it looks like a deformed finger too. Look at the fat little one." Turning my attention to the chubby, wedge-shaped piece of flesh on the outer corner of my foot, I began picking at the husk of skin that almost swallowed the tiny nail.

"Oh yeah, well, watch this." Iain put his bare foot down and craned up his big toe so that it was perpendicular to the floor.

"Yuck! Put that thing down."

His smile grew even more derisive and amused as he

started moving his toe up and down. "It's one of those mailbox flags. Mail, no mail, mail, no mail," as he raised and lowered that big toe.

"Stop it, Iain!"

"You cannot possibly say that's grosser than Pudgy," he said, grabbing on to my little toe and wiggling it. "And let's not leave out the alien finger over here."

"Leave them alone! I know they're ugly, but I like my feet."

"I like them too," he said, and he kissed my fat little toe, just to prove it.

He turned and looked straight at me, and that was when I noticed the fine white salt like traceries in the corners of his eyes. "Iain—"

"What did you expect? I've never made love before."

"Me neither."

"I have one more favor to ask you."

"Whatever you need, Sweets."

"Come with me to Sepia?"

"You're going to work? Now?"

"I'm supposed to be there anyway. Please come with me? You don't have to stay for the whole time. Just come for a little while. Please? I'll give you any book you want. You can have two."

As I am bending to look at poetry books he comes up behind me, touching my hip with a quick hand before moving off to take inventory of the philosophy section, and though he never faces me I know he sees the smile break over my face like day.

Iain at work, serious, reticent, lissome as he moves from task to task. He threads his olive scent through the circuitous bookstore like the ant in the conch. His voice is different: flat and controlled as he responds to customers' queries over the telephone, but in the dimness of the store he sparkles like goldstone.

Iain was with me in Sullivan Fields, my birthday, blueberry season. It was not the hottest day of that summer, but it might as well have been. We had stood for hours in that ferocious heat that clung like grains of sand to sea-wet skin, shaded by the brims of obnoxious straw hats. Moving slowly along the rows of twisting green and beaten-down brown, we had scouted for those tiny fruits, tiny islands in a relentless striped sea. With a basket of berries beside us, we were lying on our backs now, first spread-eagled like snow angels in the grass, then head to head and our arms at 45-degree angles to our straight bodies so we formed two arrows. Ants covered our legs like an itchy blanket, and in my weariness I could swear I saw two suns, or rather one sun dividing like a cell in mitosis. As Iain was brushing sweat-clinging wisps of hair from his face with a burnt hand, he gasped and leapt up.

"What?" I said.

"I just remembered, I have one more picture left."

"You have your camera with you? Now? You've been lugging that monster this whole time, in this heat?"

"Actually yes. And I'm taking you."

"Oh no you're not. I'm a nasty sweat-hog in a straw hat." But even then I was sitting up and combing my fingers through the knots in my hair.

"You look cute. Eat blueberries and pretend I'm not here," said half of a face as the hands attached to it fixed the focus.

I stuffed my mouth with a handful of marble-sized blueberries, then said through them, "Take a blurry one at lea—"

Click.

I swallowed. "Okay, Iain, you got your shot." He was returning his camera to his backpack, brushing himself off, standing up. I watched this in confusion. "Where are you going?"

"Back."

"We're eating blueberries. We're hanging out."

"I need to develop," Iain said, starting back.

"Now?" Catching up, even a short distance, was difficult on such a hot afternoon.

"I love to develop."

"Well, if I were as talented as you are I'd want to see the finished work immediately too. Let's go."

"You know, Dana, you need to try the darkroom sometime. I like the way my skin looks under the red light. And I love the moment when the paper just begins to show signs of something. And the smell of developer on my hands."

I looked at Iain and knew that there were many kinds of soul mates.

Plodding back across the sticky fields with Iain I murmured, "A day as hot as honey."

"Oh, that reminds me," Iain said groggily. "My dad sent me a huge jar of honey. When I told him you like to go apple-picking and that you're Jewish he said something about apples and honey on Jewish New Year. We can celebrate together."

"Okay. You know Rosh Hashana is not for a few months, right?"

"Oh. Well, you should see this jar. I don't think we'll run out before then."

"How does your dad even know about apples and honey?"

"My dad knows a lot of things," Iain said dismissively.

"Mine too."

"My dad also said in his letter that he's happy I know you. He wants to meet you."

"Does he?"

"He'll probably come to DC in the fall. He'd come sooner but he hates the humidity."

"Hot as honey," I repeated.

"You know, little Dana, it's not just my dad. I'm also happy I know you."

"I'm happy I know you, Iain."

"Do you know me?"

"I don't know. I used to think you were my angel."

"An angel!" he laughed. "Do angels snort cocaine?"

"Then I thought you were made up."

"Maybe I am," he said.

"Maybe you are," I forced myself to agree. "But at least I'm not the one writing the story."

"And what if you were? How would you end it?"

Anticipation like centipedes tickles at their skins as they extend their little fingers toward each other and touch for the first time, one point of infinite energy in infinite space. The nagging question finally has an answer: "Who are you? Who are you?" I am this. I am this simple point of truth, powerful solvent of artifice. Her muscles ache from defeating a stone-dwelling ghost.

The thick stink of what-I-want and what-you-want. What do I want? Only this, she says, touching the tip of his little finger with the tip of hers. When we touch we do not really touch. The molecules of my body will not reach the interstices of yours. What is it then that I feel when my fingertip aligns with yours? A current of energy, a hot blue thread of ions, a spiritual surge experienced as a change of polarity in the synapses. The brain transforms this into the experience of touch, of heat and pressure, and again we alter the sensation as we interpret. But first we have this point of truthful contact—the understanding that at last it is you that I love. That I am no longer content to sleep in the arms of a lover I created. The particles of my body dissociate for an unfathomable instant and I am light, inside you, moving ichor in your veins. That is what I mean when I say I love you: that we are in each other, that we know how to touch, that our tenuous and tenacious link has a fertile presence in this momentary world.

Acknowledgements

Thanking is difficult. The people who stuck with me and believed in me through the writing of this book deserve so much more than this lousy page, but it's what I've got, so here we go. I thank my Mom, my Dad, my brothers Stephen and Marc, and *di ganze mishpuchah* by blood and by bread. I thank the women: Taal McLean, Sara Morse, Julie Kay Philips, Amy Goorin, and Susana Espasa Guerrero. The most patient and helpful readers of my crappy first draft, Manny Guerrero and Christopher Renino, get my gratitude and big karma points. I thank every teacher who ever bothered to teach me, most especially Audrey Strauss, Paul Sheehey, Trevor Nightingale, John Aune, Joe Algrant, and of course Lawrence E. Mitchell. Without the help of Michael Golder there might not have been a me to write the book, and I hope that now he'll read the thing. Ira Wood and Marge Piercy have been truly wonderful and their insightful commentary has helped me make my work better. And my profound thanks go to Aninaggen, for falling on her knee; to Larry, my life, my light, my reason; and to the warrior, Marilyn Freiman, whose love defeated death. I wish she could have lived to see this.

The Author

Lauren Porosoff Mitchell received her degree in English from Wesleyan University and her law degree from George Washington University. She lives in Washington, D.C. with her family, where she teaches and is at work on her second novel.